MORE PRAISE FOR BABYMOUSE!

"Sassy, smart . . .
Babymouse is here
to stay."
—The Horn Book Magazine

"Young readers
will happily
fall in line."
—Kirkus Reviews

"The brother-sister creative team hits the mark
with humor, sweetness, and characters so genuine
they can pass for real kids." —Booklist

"Babymouse is spunky, ambitious,
and, at times, a total dweeb."
—School Library Journal

Be sure to read **all** the **BABYMOUSE** books:

#1 BABYMOUSE: Queen of the World!
#2 BABYMOUSE: Our Hero
#3 BABYMOUSE: Beach Babe
#4 BABYMOUSE: Rock Star
#5 BABYMOUSE: Heartbreaker
#6 CAMP BABYMOUSE
#7 BABYMOUSE: Skater Girl
#8 BABYMOUSE: Puppy Love
#9 BABYMOUSE: Monster Mash
#10 BABYMOUSE: The Musical
#11 BABYMOUSE: Dragonslayer
#12 BABYMOUSE: Burns Rubber
#13 BABYMOUSE: Cupcake Tycoon
#14 BABYMOUSE: Mad Scientist
#15 A Very BABYMOUSE Christmas
#16 BABYMOUSE for President
#17 EXTREME BABYMOUSE

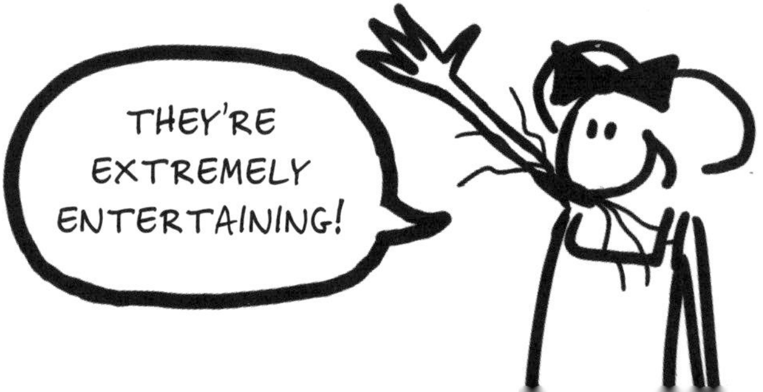
THEY'RE EXTREMELY ENTERTAINING!

EXTREME
BABYMOUSE

BY JENNIFER L. HOLM & MATTHEW HOLM

RANDOM HOUSE 🏠 NEW YORK

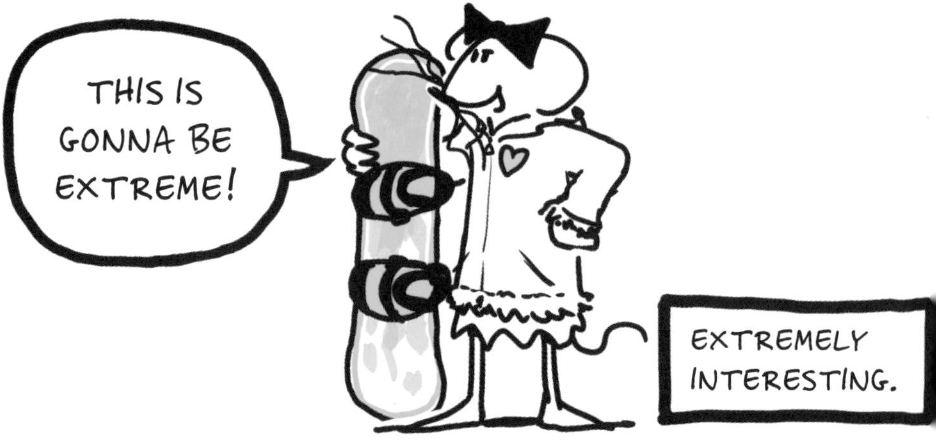
THIS IS GONNA BE EXTREME!
EXTREMELY INTERESTING.

Special thanks to Jarrett Krosoczka for Lunch Lady's guest appearance.

Visit us on the Web!
randomhouse.com/kids
Babymouse.com

Educators and librarians, for a variety of teaching tools, visit us at RHTeachersLibrarians.com

Library of Congress Cataloging-in-Publication Data
Holm, Jennifer L.
Extreme Babymouse / by Jennifer L. Holm & Matthew Holm. — 1st ed.
p. cm. — (Babymouse ; #17)
Summary: It seems that everyone at school has taken up snowboarding, so Babymouse decides she must hit the slopes, too.
1. Graphic novels. [1. Graphic novels. 2. Imagination—Fiction. 3. Snowboarding—Fiction. 4. Schools—Fiction. 5. Mice—Fiction.] I. Holm, Matthew. II. Title.
PZ7.7.H65Ext 2013 741.5'9—dc23 2012022834

ISBN 978-0-307-93160-3 (trade) — ISBN 978-0-375-97096-2 (lib. bdg.) — ISBN 978-0-307-97543-0 (ebook)

MANUFACTURED IN MALAYSIA 10 9 8 7 6 5 4 3 2 1 First Edition

Random House Children's Books supports the First Amendment and celebrates the right to read.

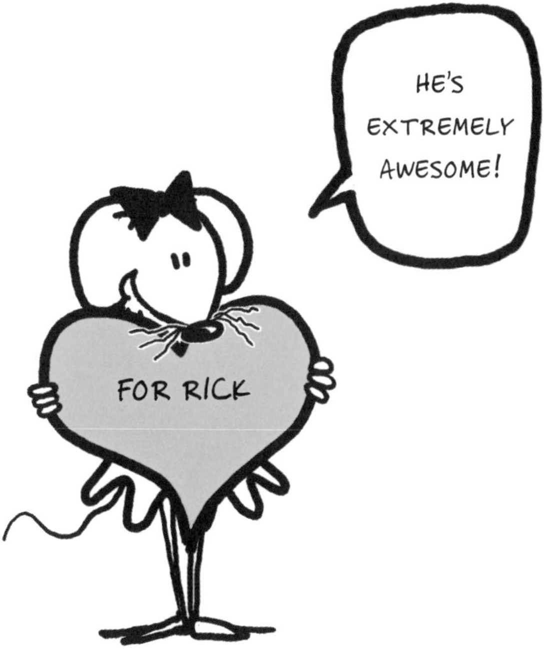
HE'S EXTREMELY AWESOME!
FOR RICK

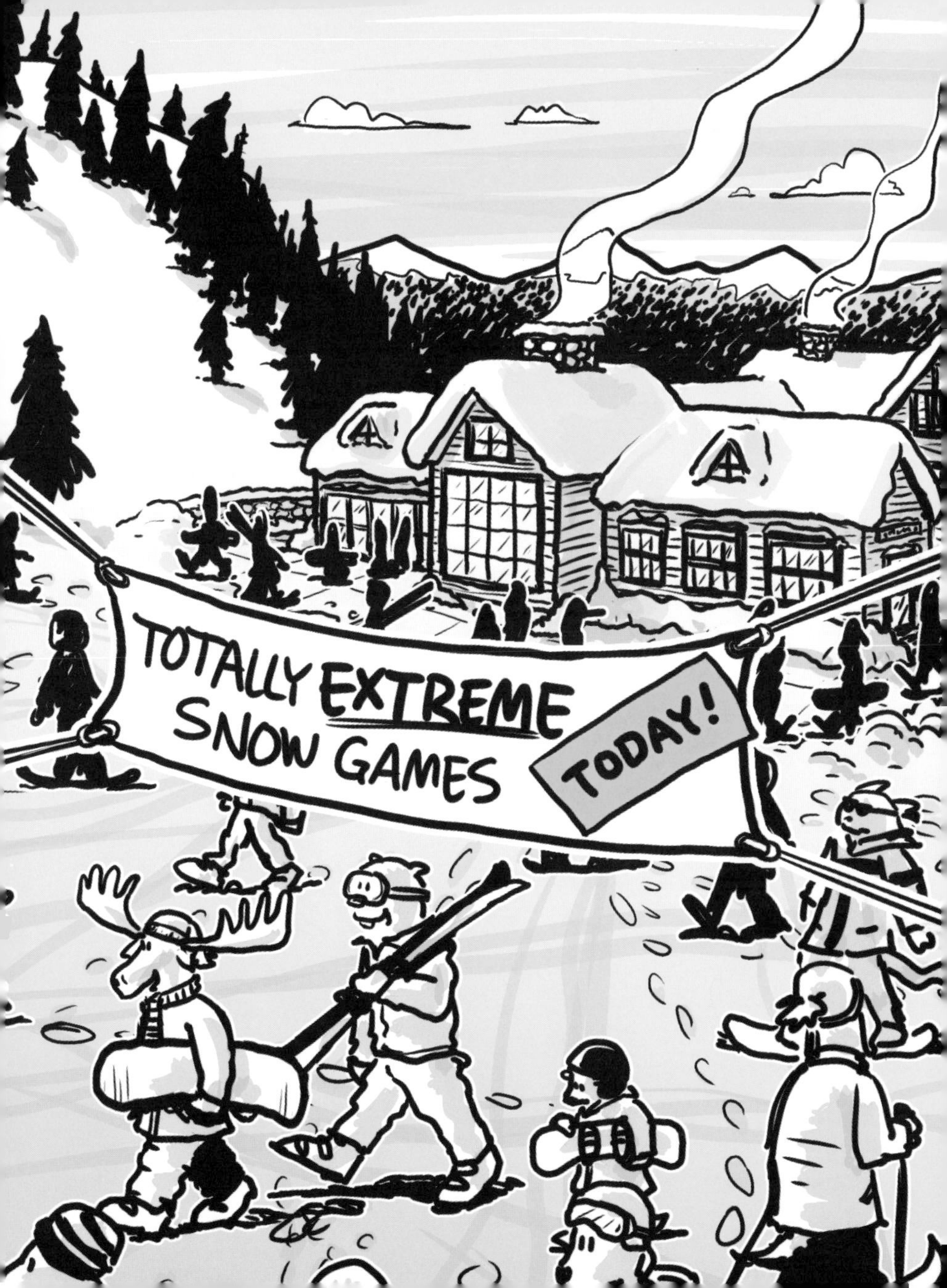
TOTALLY EXTREME
SNOW GAMES
TODAY!

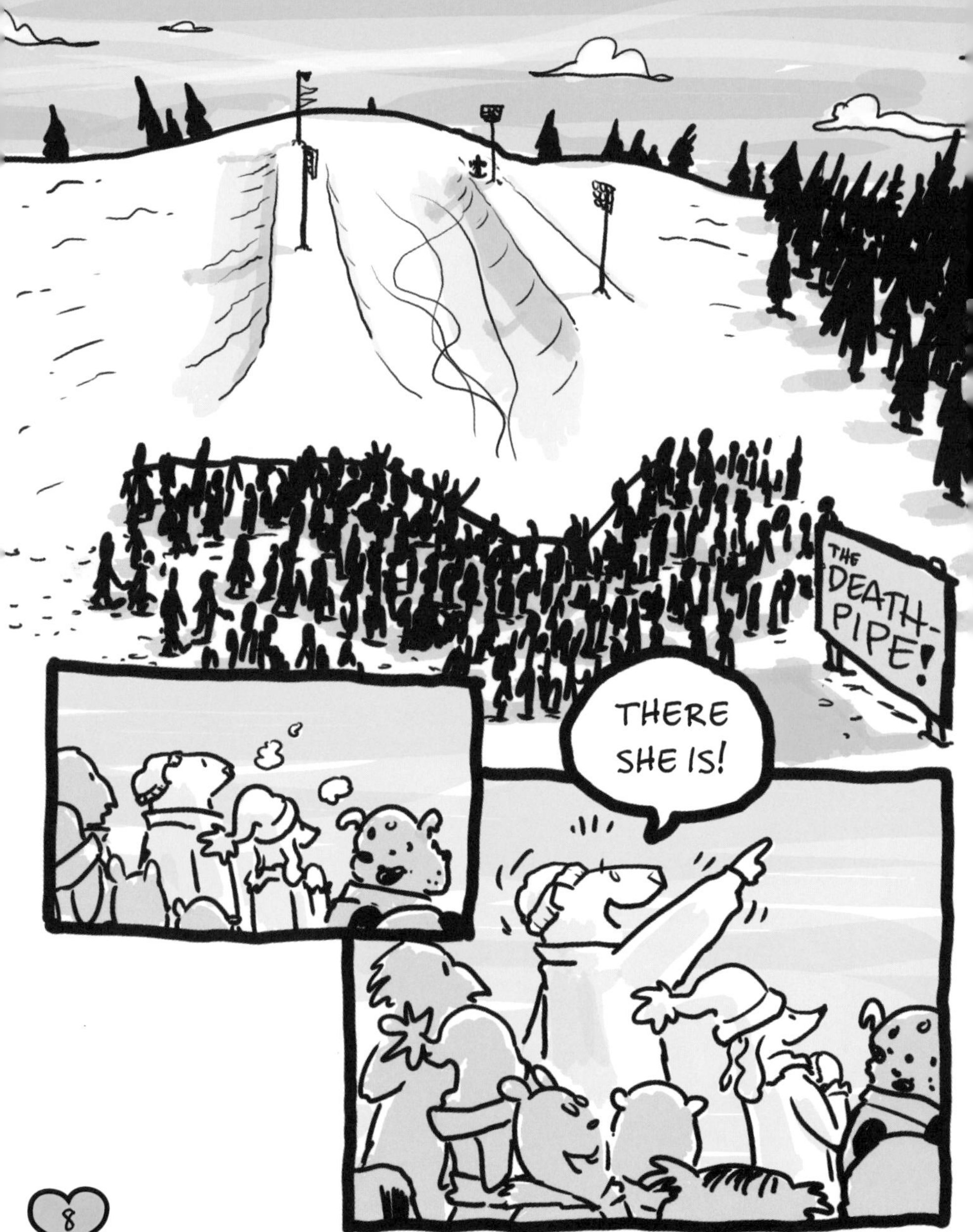
THE DEATH-PIPE!
THERE SHE IS!

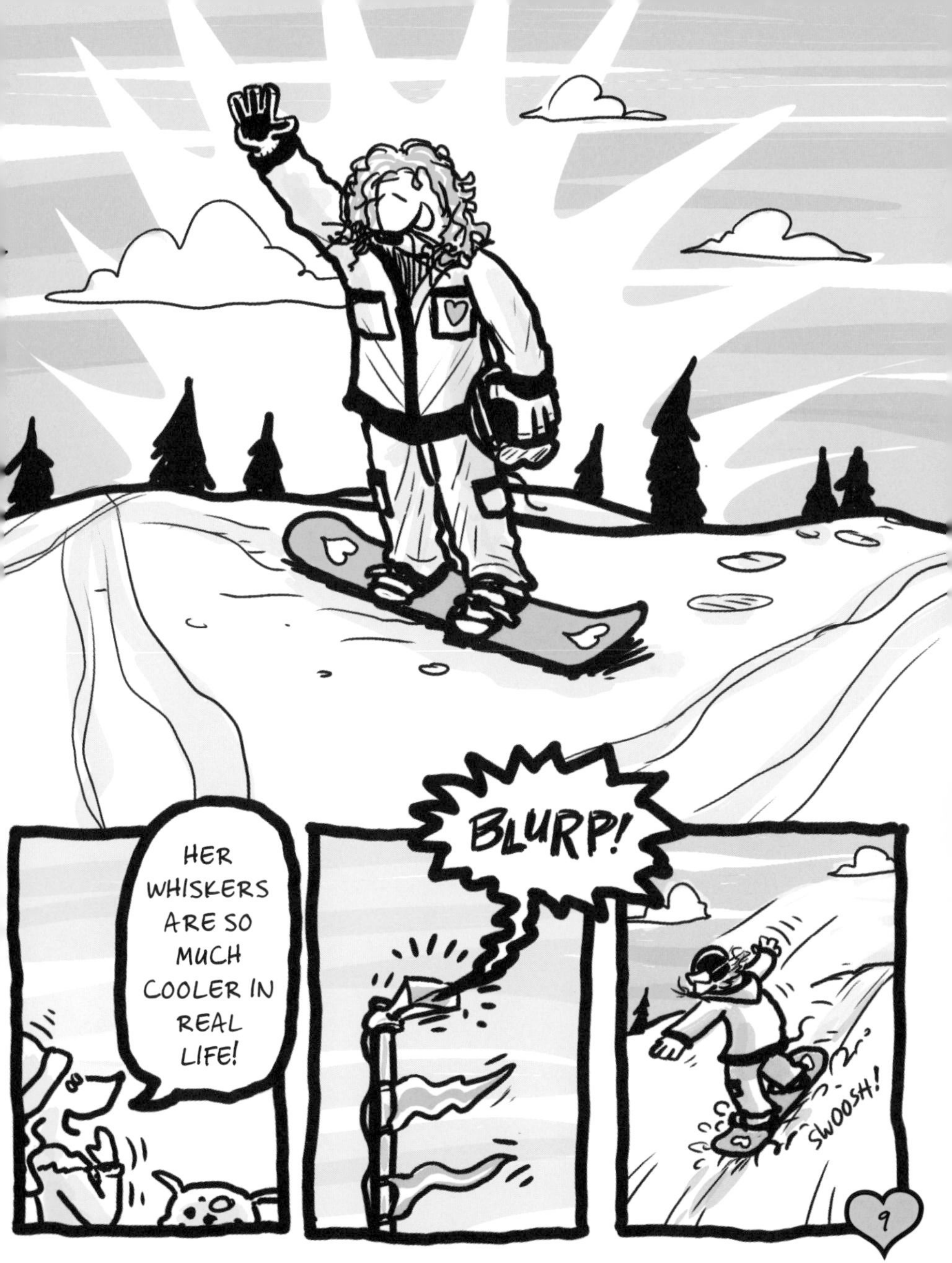
HER WHISKERS ARE SO MUCH COOLER IN REAL LIFE!
BLURP!
SWOOSH!

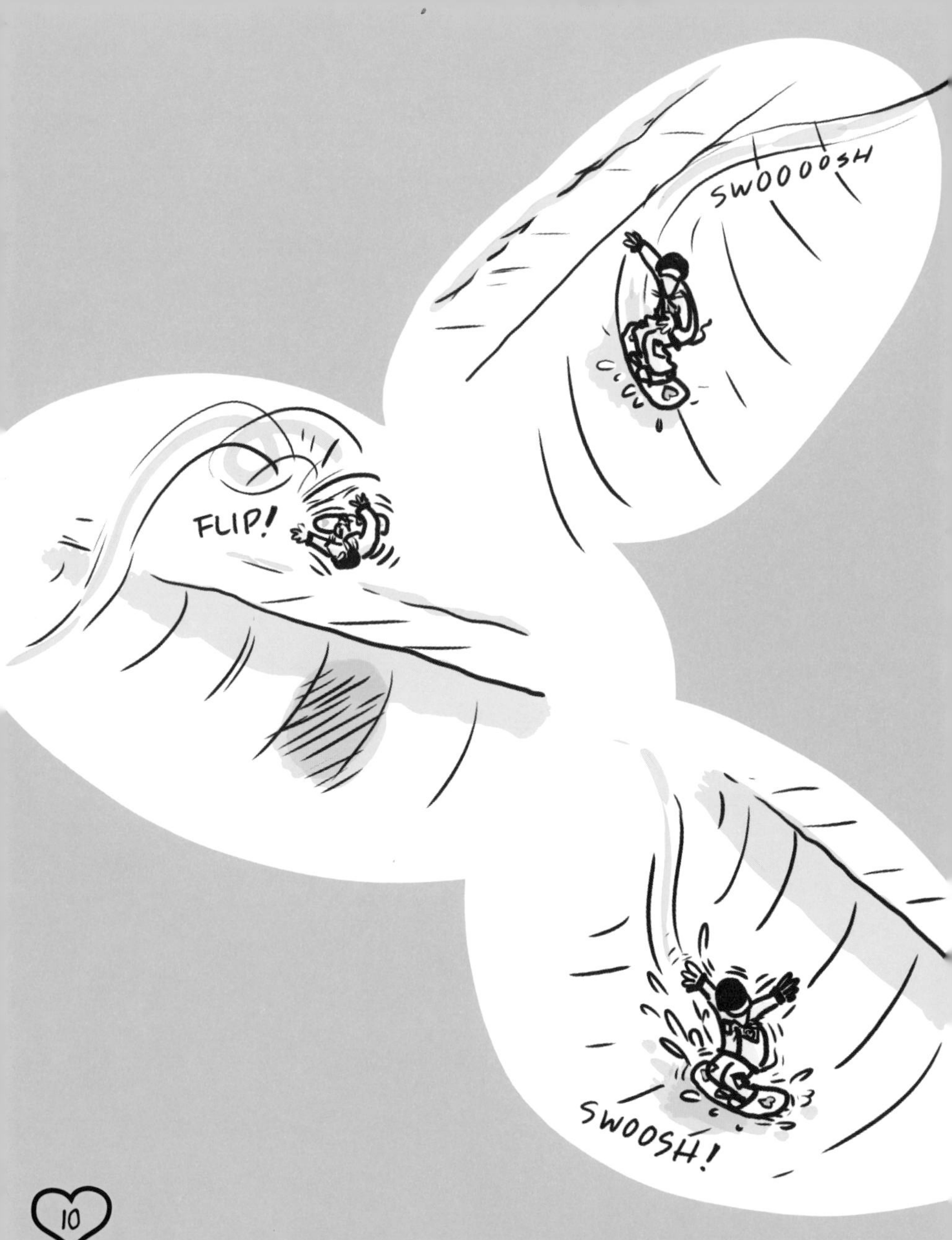
SWOOOOSH
FLIP!
SWOOSH!

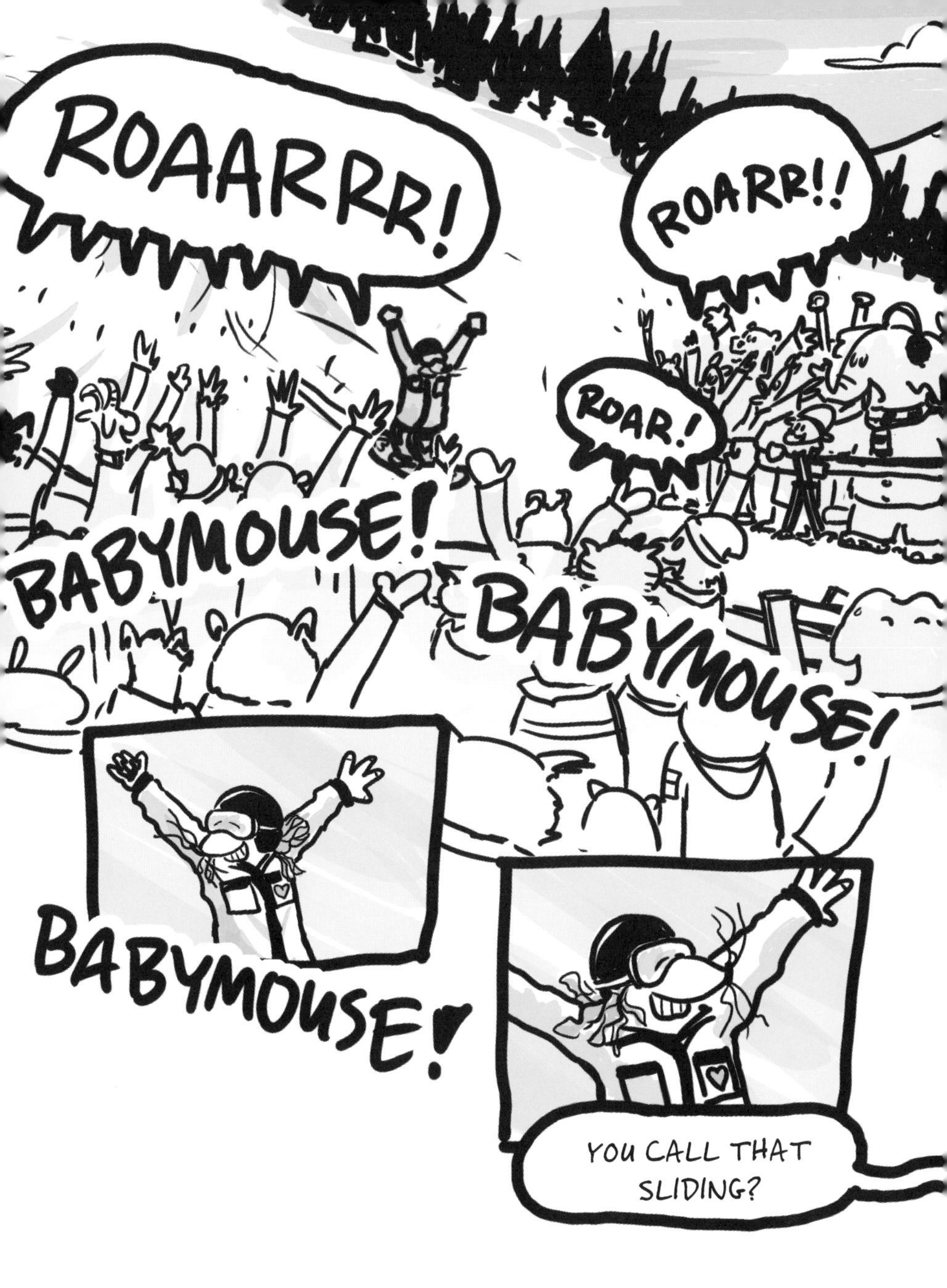
ROAARRR!
ROARR!!
ROAR!
BABYMOUSE!
BABYMOUSE!
BABYMOUSE!
YOU CALL THAT SLIDING?

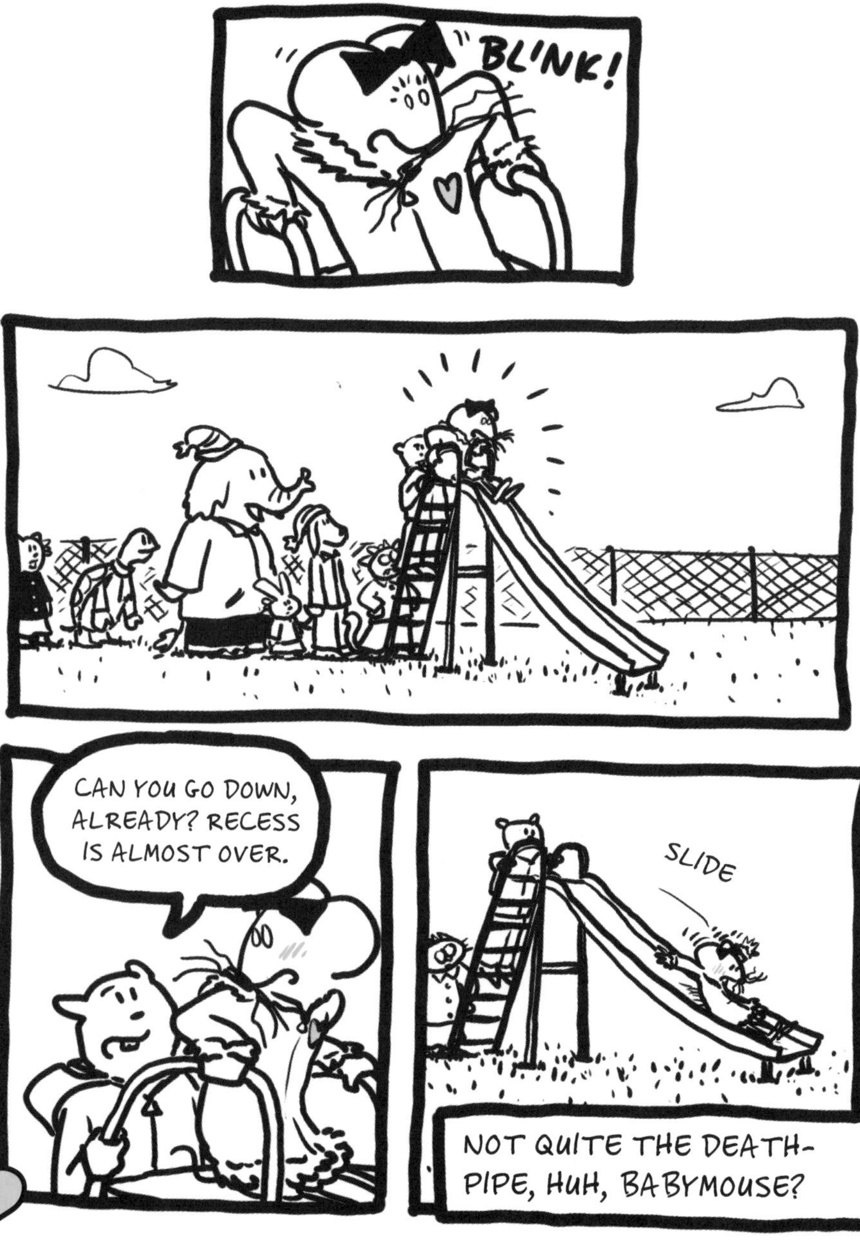
BLINK!
CAN YOU GO DOWN, ALREADY? RECESS IS ALMOST OVER.
SLIDE
NOT QUITE THE DEATH-PIPE, HUH, BABYMOUSE?

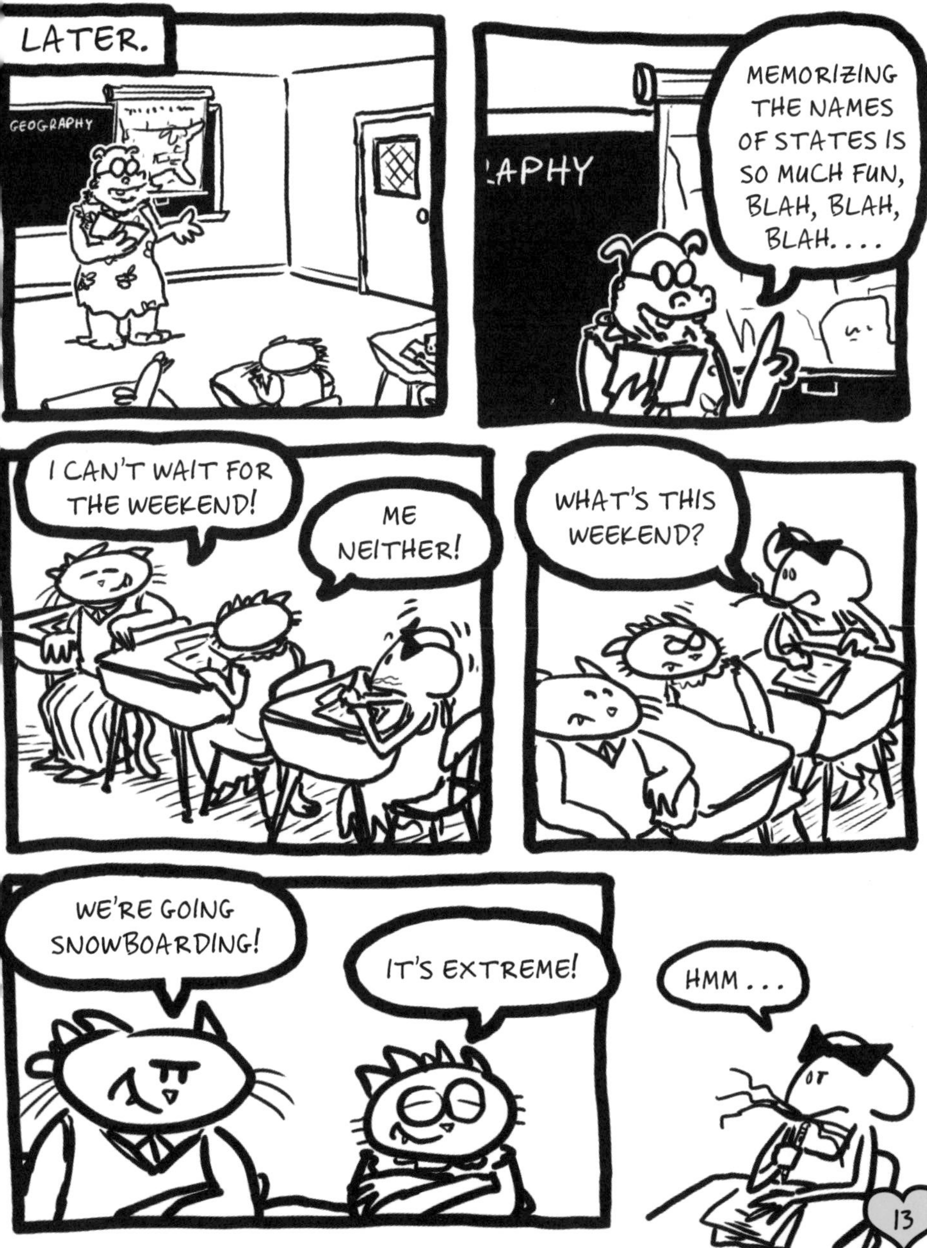
LATER.
GEOGRAPHY
MEMORIZING THE NAMES OF STATES IS SO MUCH FUN, BLAH, BLAH, BLAH. . . .
I CAN'T WAIT FOR THE WEEKEND!
ME NEITHER!
WHAT'S THIS WEEKEND?
WE'RE GOING SNOWBOARDING!
IT'S EXTREME!
HMM . . .

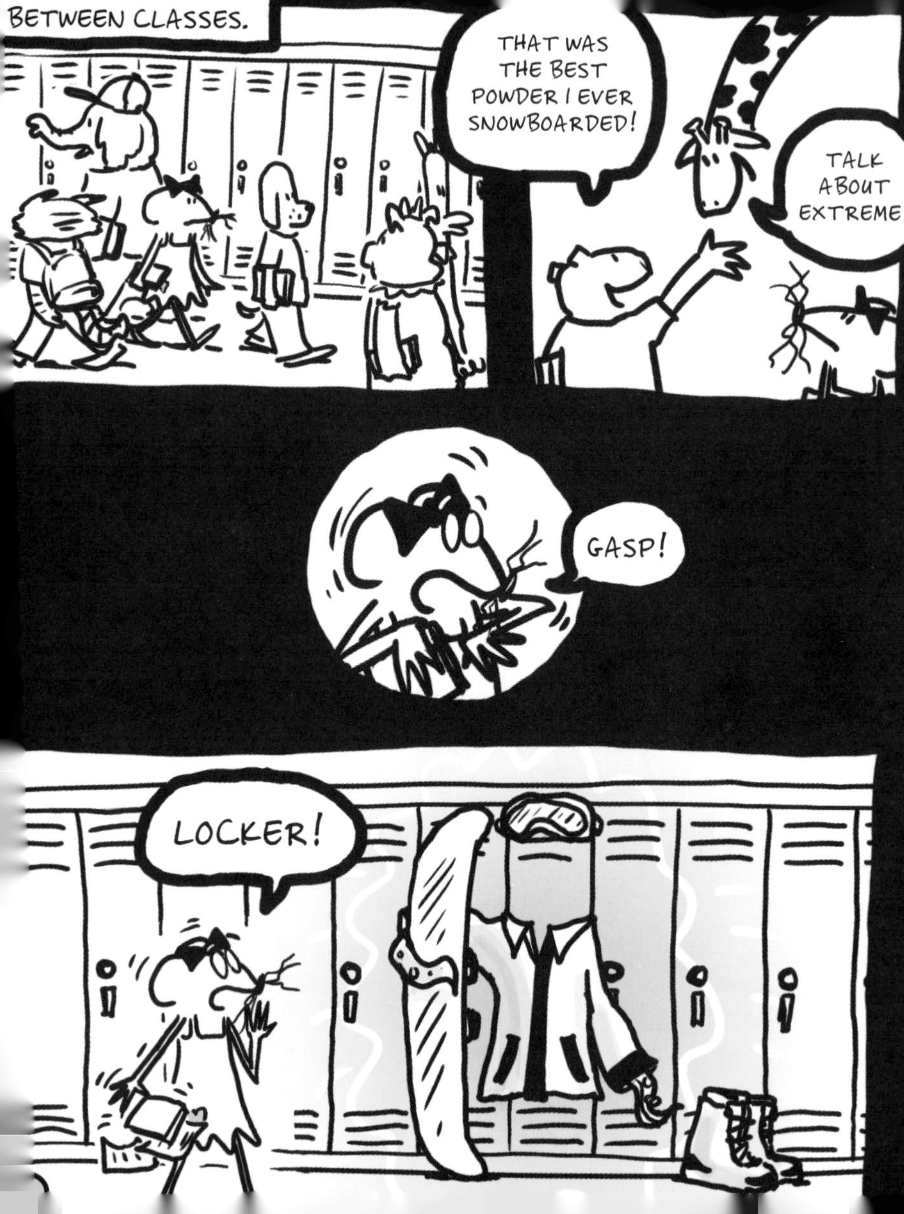
BETWEEN CLASSES.
THAT WAS THE BEST POWDER I EVER SNOWBOARDED!
TALK ABOUT EXTREME!
GASP!
LOCKER!

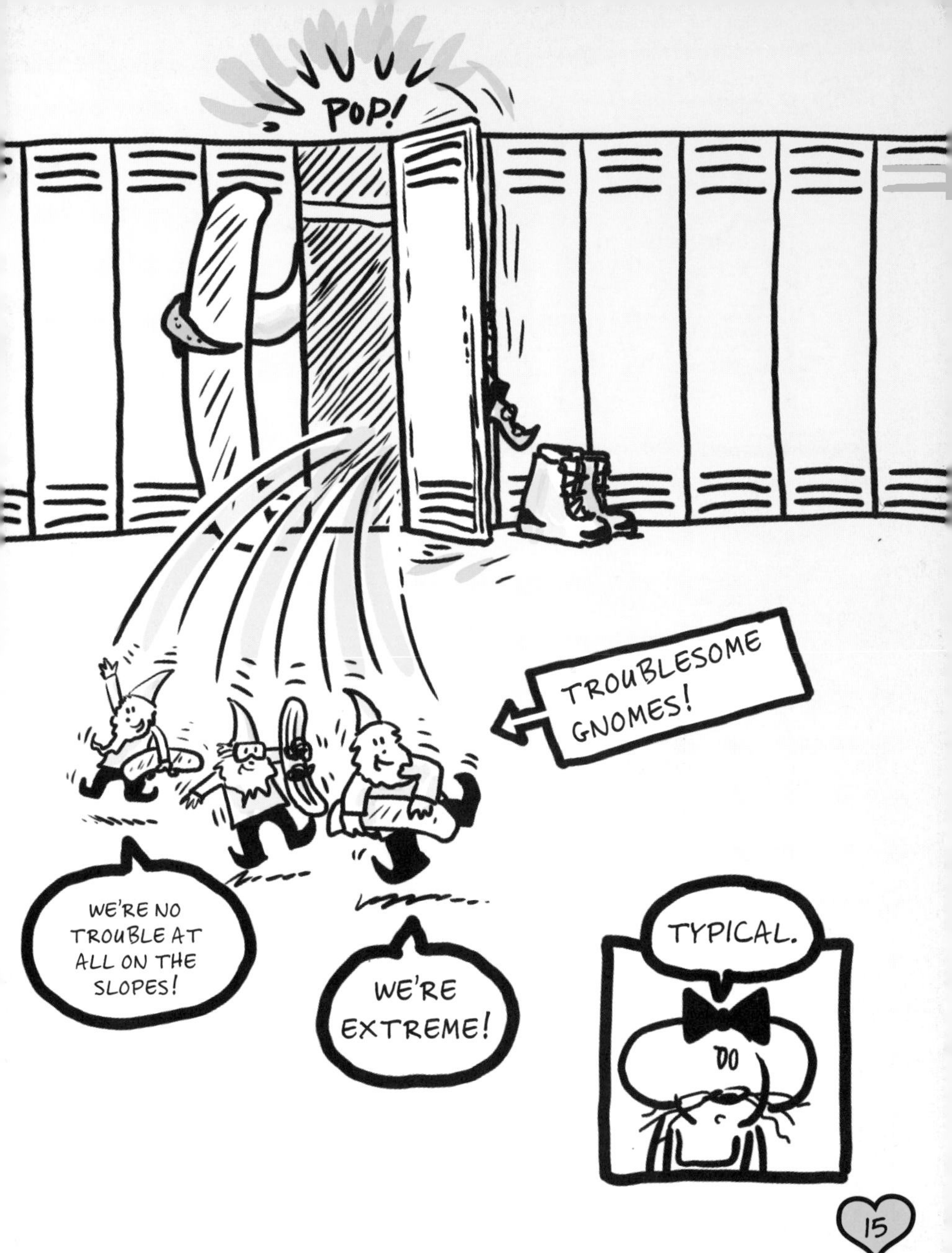
POP!
TROUBLESOME GNOMES!
WE'RE NO TROUBLE AT ALL ON THE SLOPES!
WE'RE EXTREME!
TYPICAL.

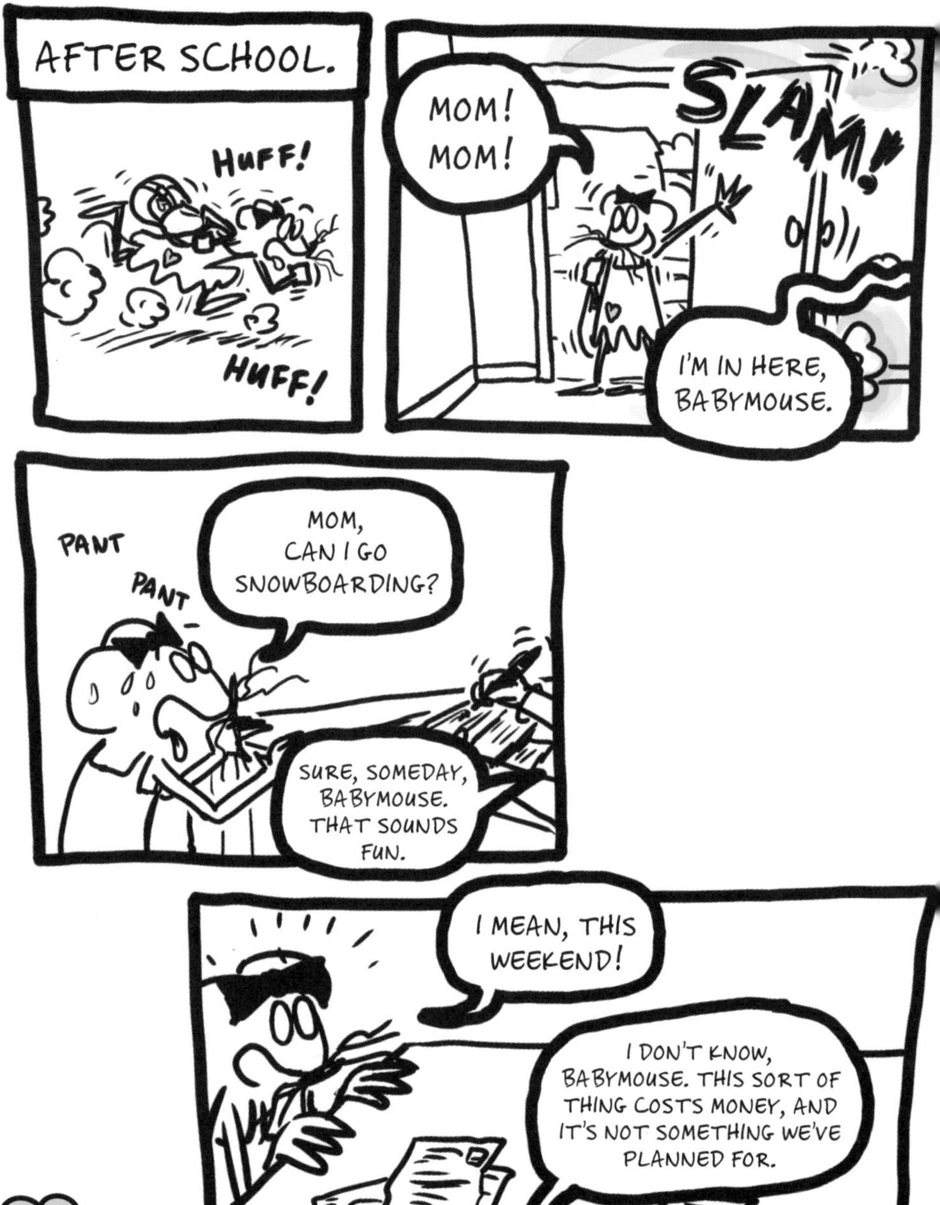
AFTER SCHOOL.
HUFF!
HUFF!
MOM! MOM!
SLAM!
I'M IN HERE, BABYMOUSE.
PANT
PANT
MOM, CAN I GO SNOWBOARDING?
SURE, SOMEDAY, BABYMOUSE. THAT SOUNDS FUN.
I MEAN, THIS WEEKEND!
I DON'T KNOW, BABYMOUSE. THIS SORT OF THING COSTS MONEY, AND IT'S NOT SOMETHING WE'VE PLANNED FOR.

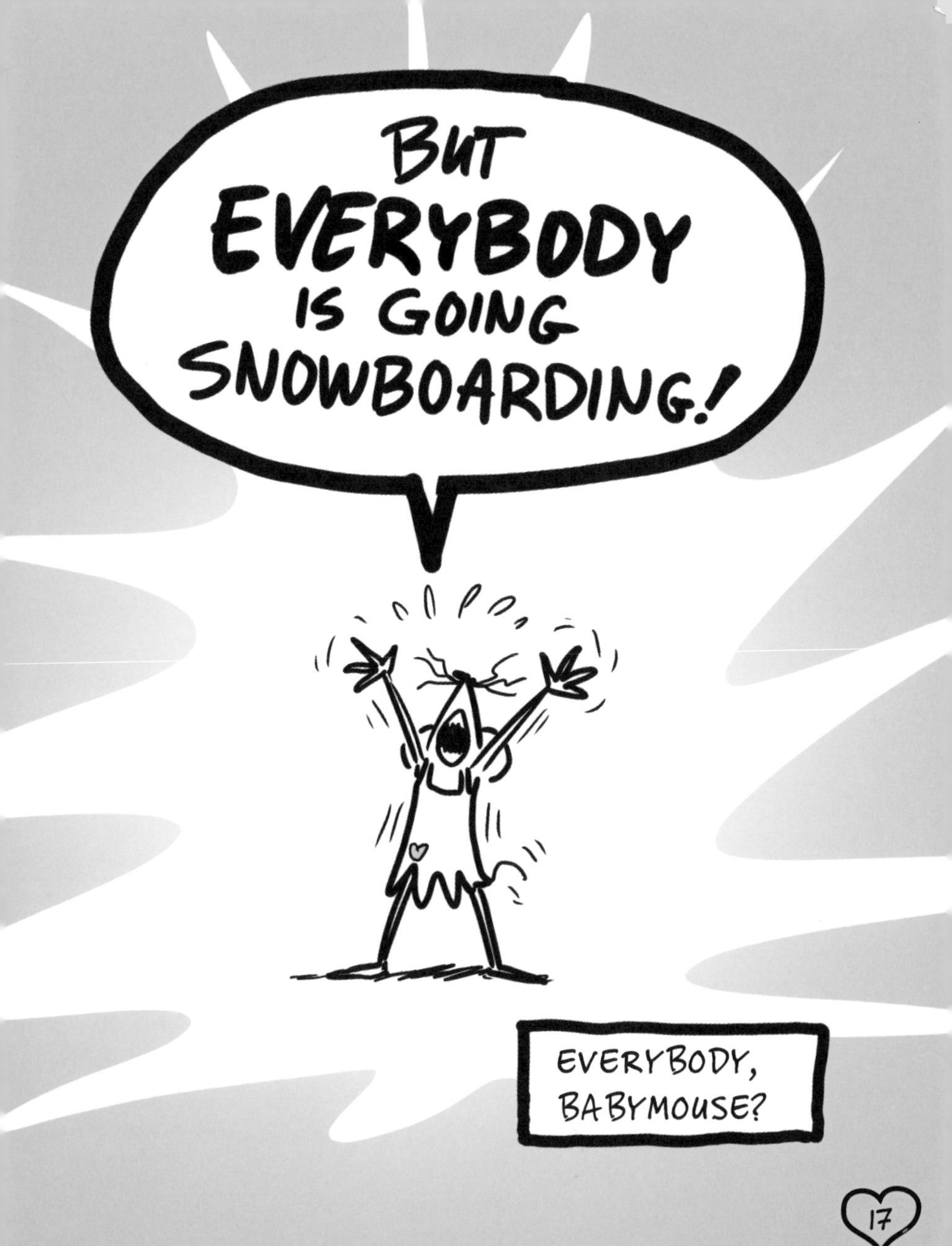
BUT EVERYBODY IS GOING SNOWBOARDING!
EVERYBODY, BABYMOUSE?

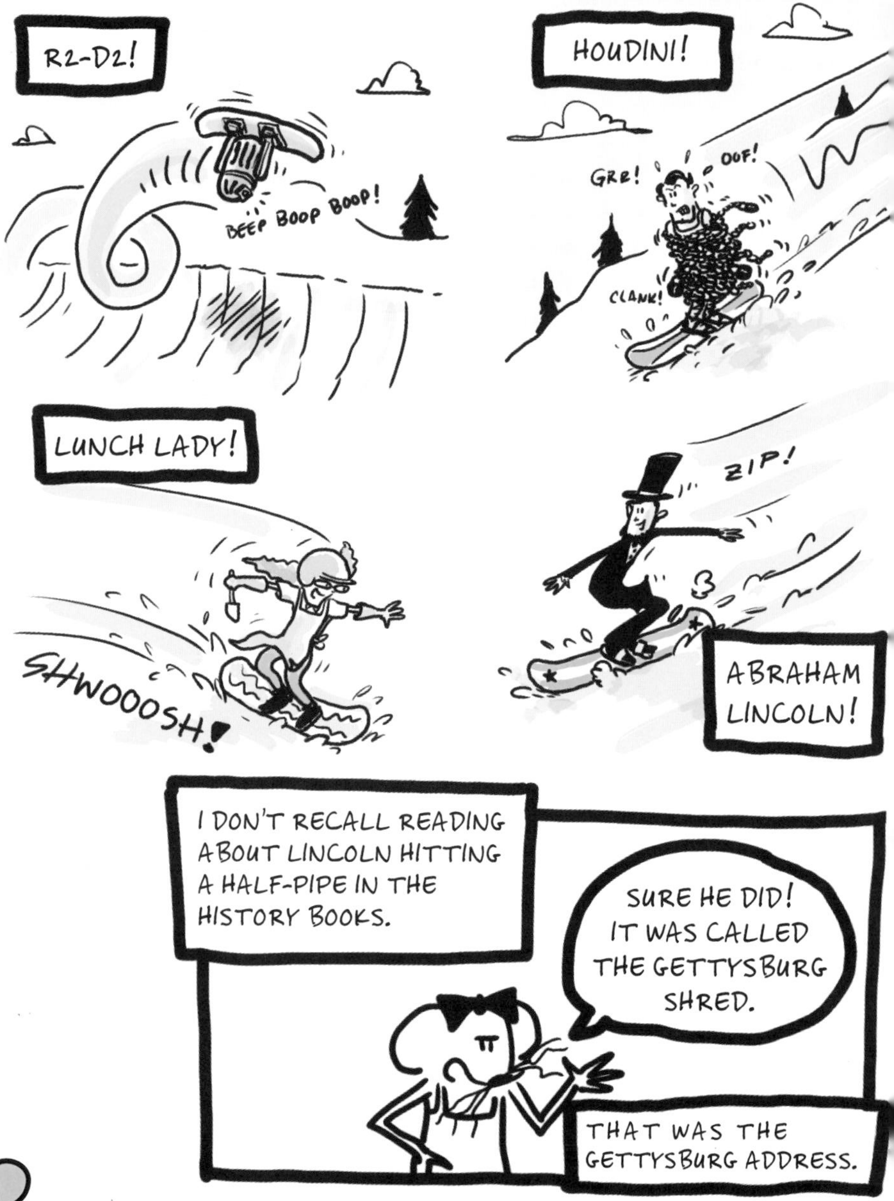
R2-D2!
BEEP BOOP BOOP!
HOUDINI!
GRR!
OOF!
CLANK!
LUNCH LADY!
SHWOOOSH!
ZIP!
ABRAHAM LINCOLN!
I DON'T RECALL READING ABOUT LINCOLN HITTING A HALF-PIPE IN THE HISTORY BOOKS.
SURE HE DID! IT WAS CALLED THE GETTYSBURG SHRED.
THAT WAS THE GETTYSBURG ADDRESS.

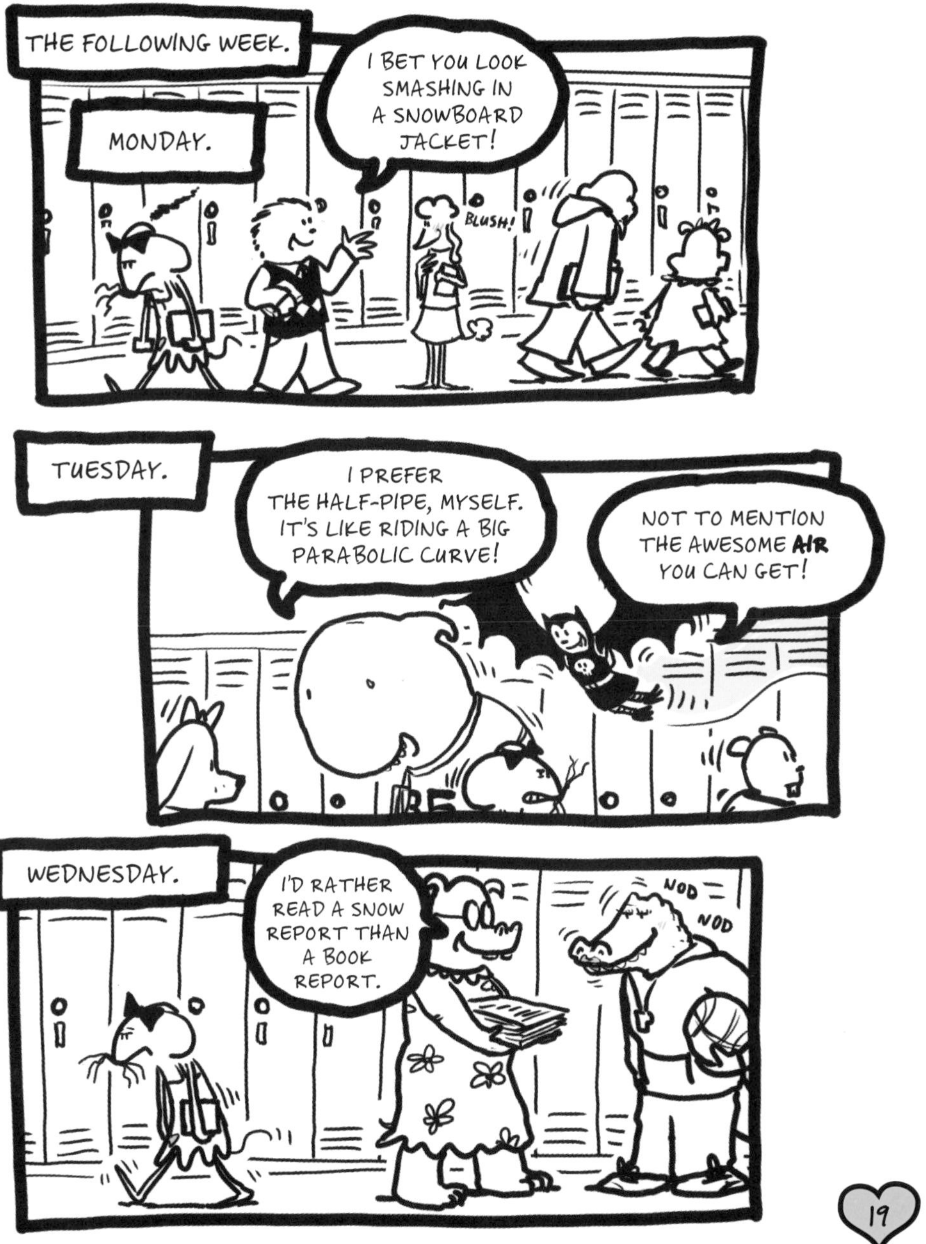

THE FOLLOWING WEEK.
MONDAY.
I BET YOU LOOK SMASHING IN A SNOWBOARD JACKET!
BLUSH!
TUESDAY.
I PREFER THE HALF-PIPE, MYSELF. IT'S LIKE RIDING A BIG PARABOLIC CURVE!
NOT TO MENTION THE AWESOME AIR YOU CAN GET!
WEDNESDAY.
I'D RATHER READ A SNOW REPORT THAN A BOOK REPORT.
NOD
NOD

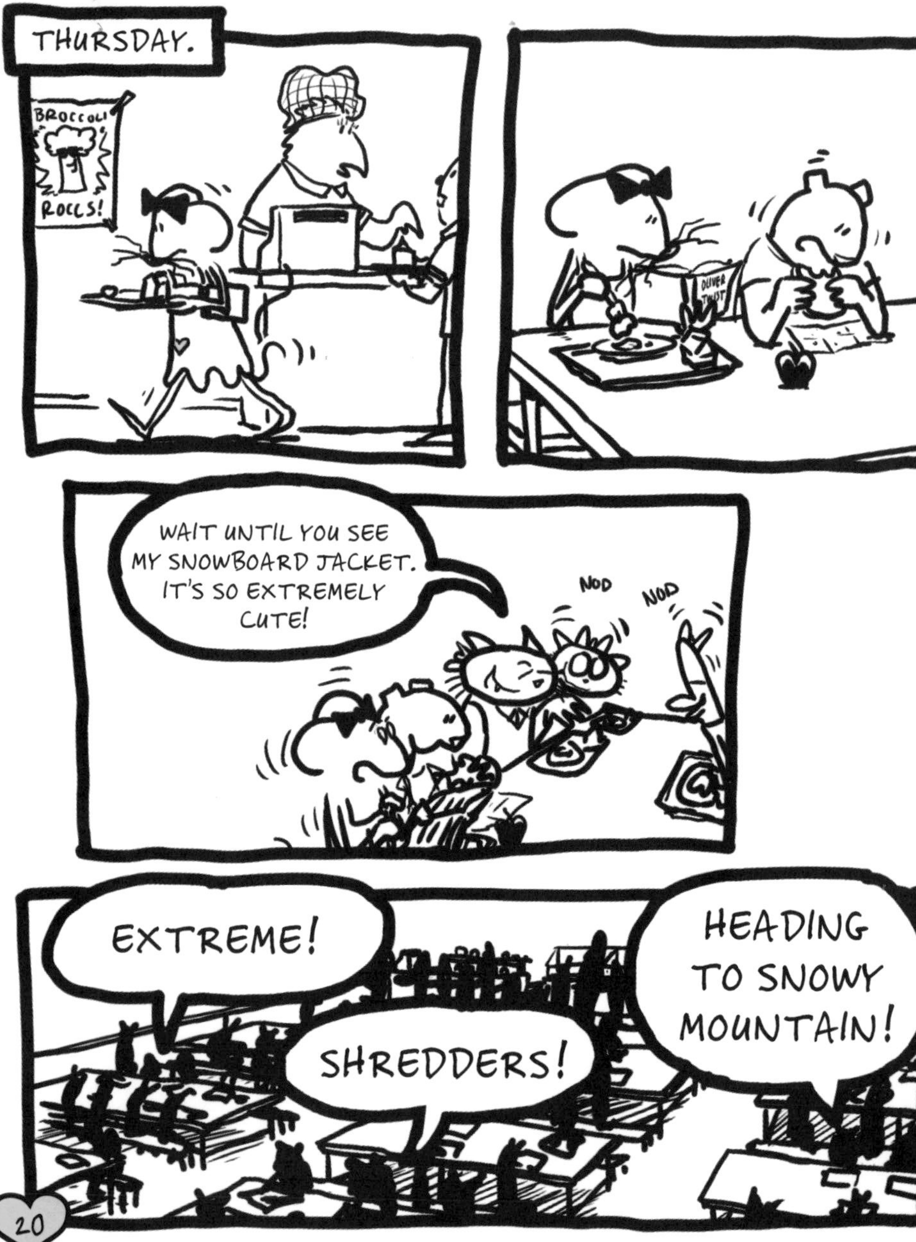
THURSDAY.
BROCCOLI ROCCS!
OLIVER TWIST
WAIT UNTIL YOU SEE MY SNOWBOARD JACKET. IT'S SO EXTREMELY CUTE!
NOD
NOD
EXTREME!
SHREDDERS!
HEADING TO SNOWY MOUNTAIN!

TREME! GET YOUR BOARD WAXED! DU

LACK DIAMOND ALL THE WAY! GONNA B

VEET, SWEET, SWEET! SHREDDERS!!!

PE CONDITIONS WILL BE EPIC! I CAN'T

AIT TO HIT THE RAILS, DUDE! NEED TO

OWDER! I'M GOOFY! WE'RE TOTALLY GO

RED THE BACKSIDE BEFORE WE HIT T

ALF-PIPE. SHE'S SUCH AN AIRDOG! TOT

XTREME! SHOULD HAVE RUN THE CHUT

AN! THAT WAS AN OLLIE YOU COULD PU

HE BOOKS! SHAVE THAT SIDE! THERE'

ONNA BE FRESHIES! DID YOU SEE HER 5

TWIST? THAT WAS SO EXTR !! TE

OU'RE READY WE'LL GET T S

XED UP AND HIT IT AT FIR !

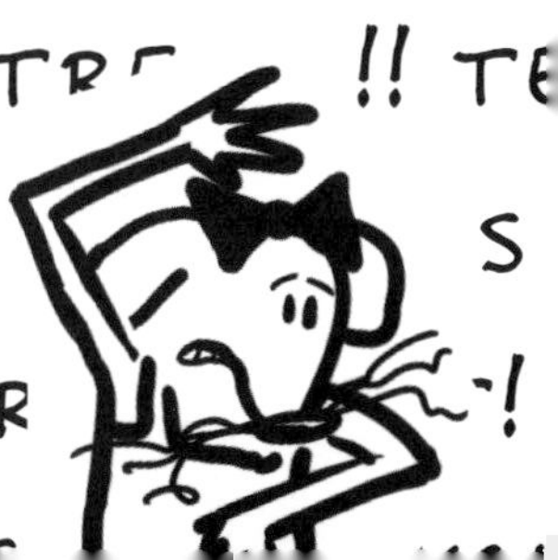

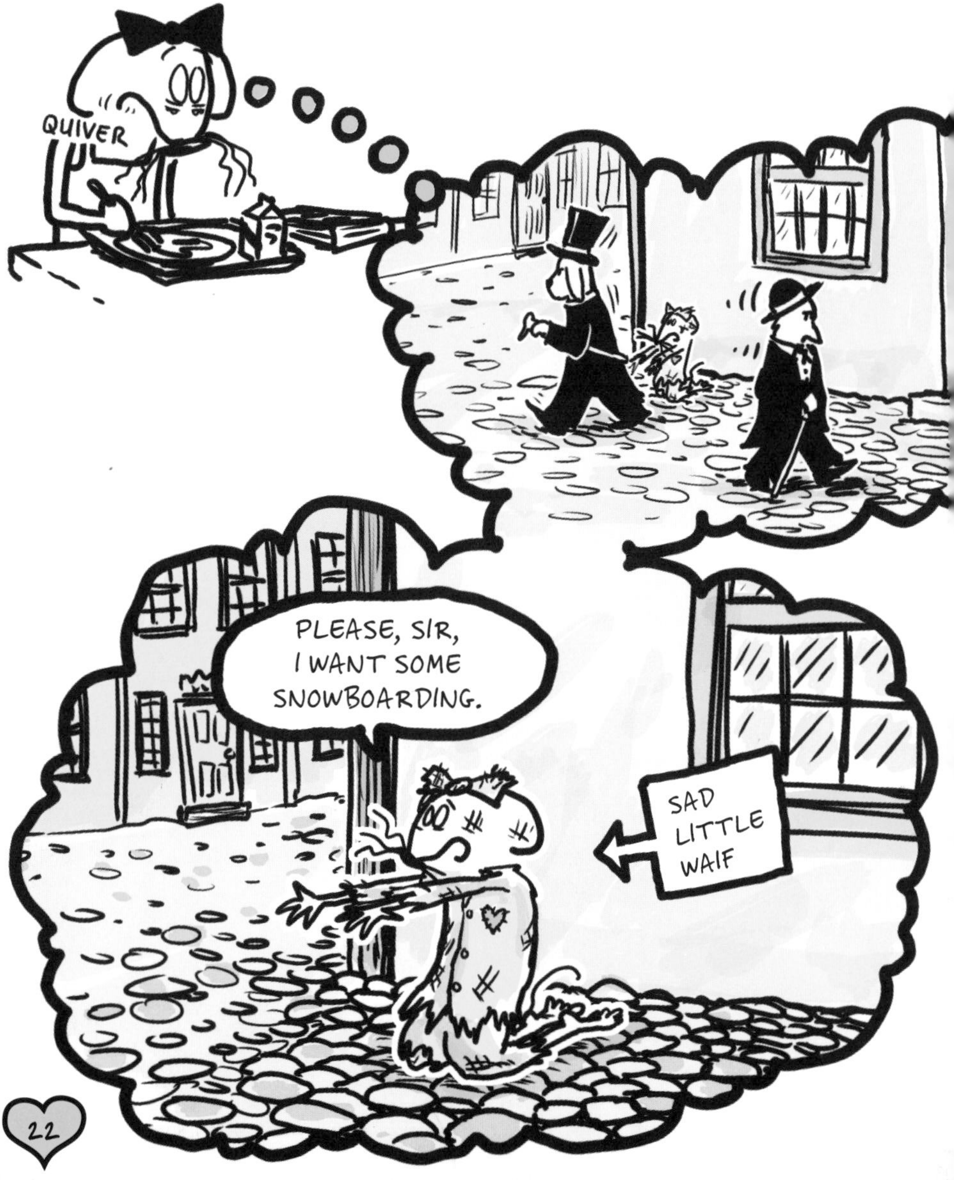
QUIVER
PLEASE, SIR, I WANT SOME SNOWBOARDING.
SAD LITTLE WAIF

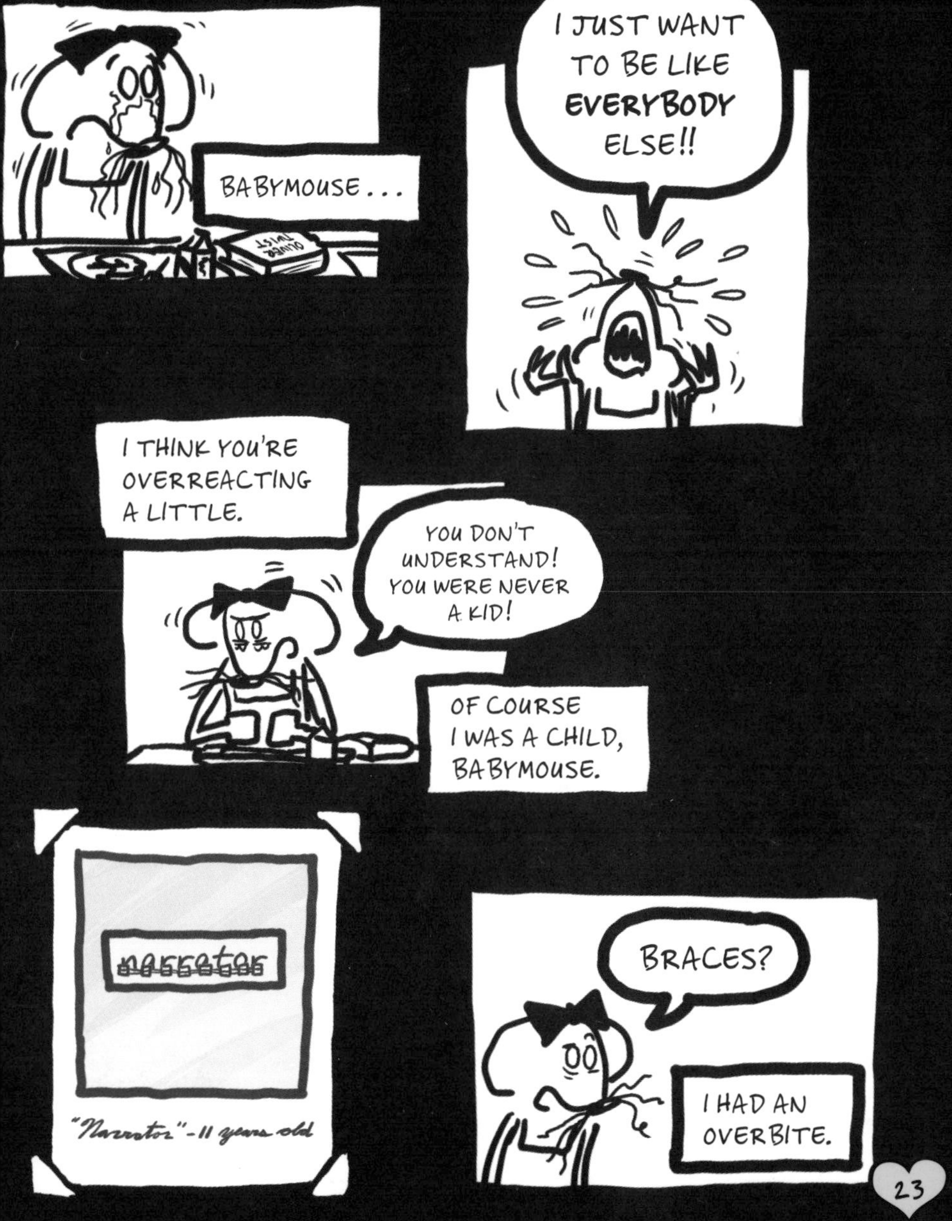
BABYMOUSE . . .
I JUST WANT TO BE LIKE **EVERYBODY** ELSE!!
OLIVER TWIST
I THINK YOU'RE OVERREACTING A LITTLE.
YOU DON'T UNDERSTAND! YOU WERE NEVER A KID!
OF COURSE I WAS A CHILD, BABYMOUSE.
narrator
"Narrator" - 11 years old
BRACES?
I HAD AN OVERBITE.

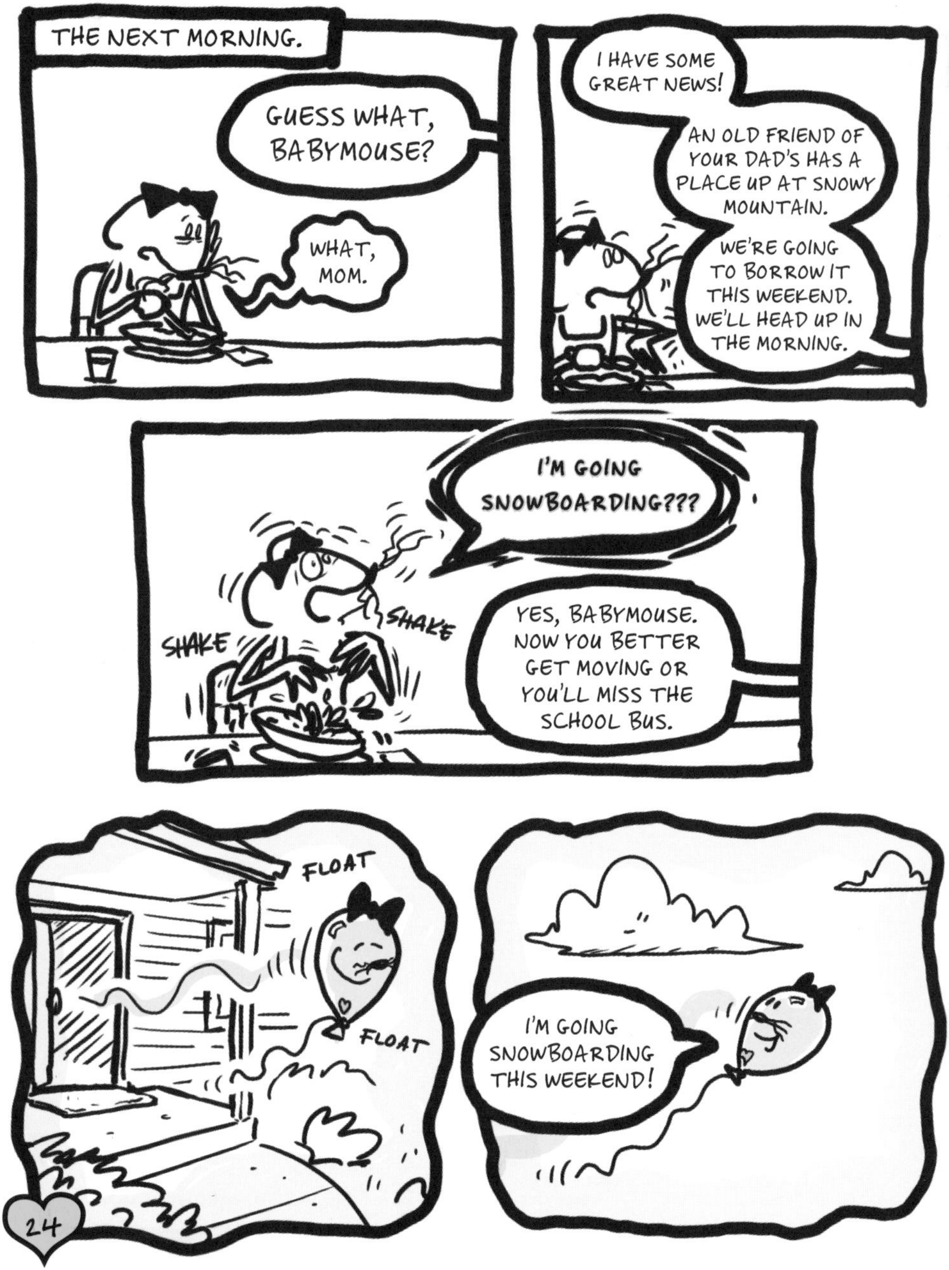
THE NEXT MORNING.
GUESS WHAT, BABYMOUSE?
WHAT, MOM.
I HAVE SOME GREAT NEWS!
AN OLD FRIEND OF YOUR DAD'S HAS A PLACE UP AT SNOWY MOUNTAIN.
WE'RE GOING TO BORROW IT THIS WEEKEND. WE'LL HEAD UP IN THE MORNING.
I'M GOING SNOWBOARDING???
SHAKE
SHAKE
YES, BABYMOUSE. NOW YOU BETTER GET MOVING OR YOU'LL MISS THE SCHOOL BUS.
FLOAT
FLOAT
I'M GOING SNOWBOARDING THIS WEEKEND!

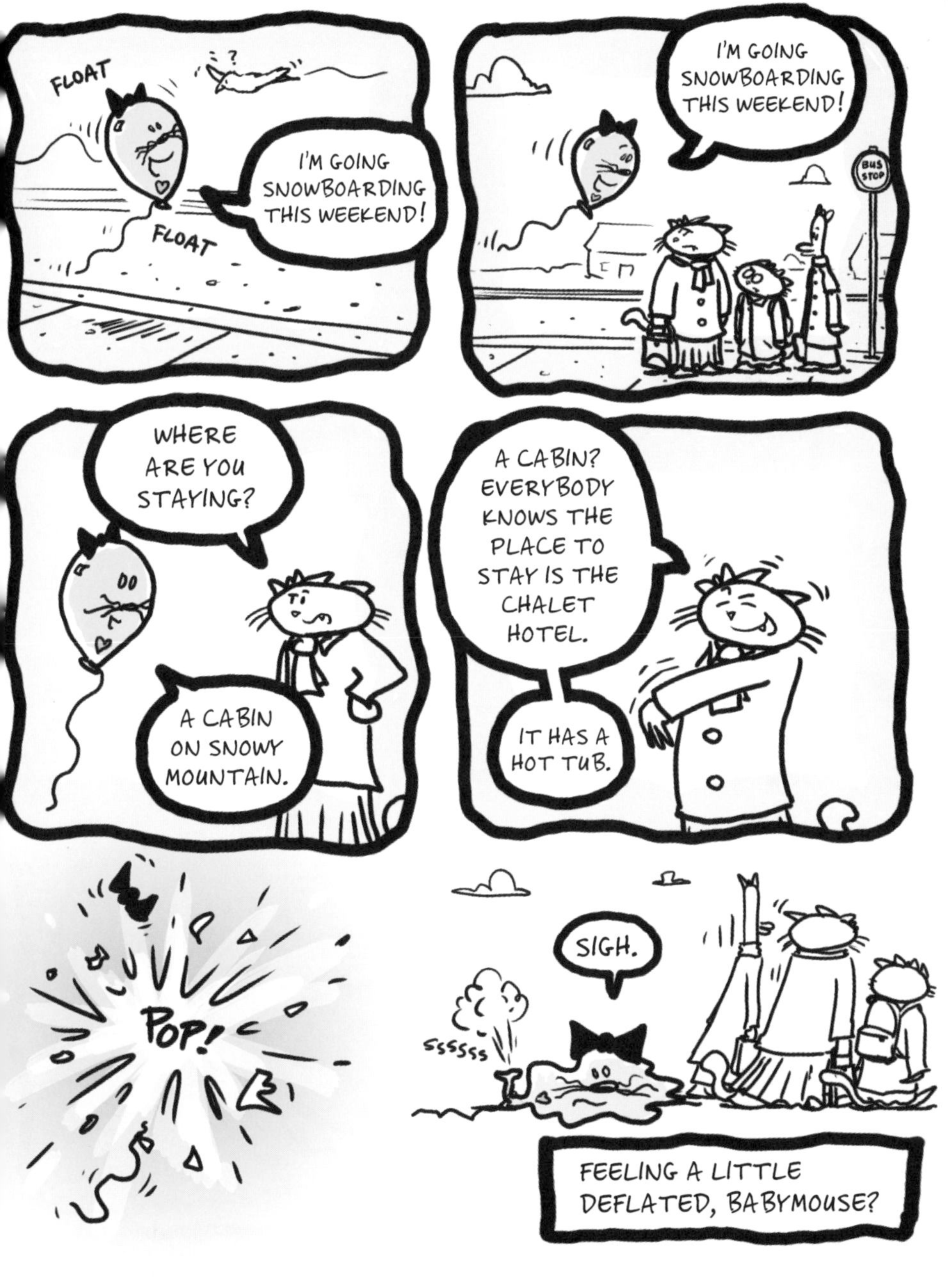
FLOAT
I'M GOING SNOWBOARDING THIS WEEKEND!
FLOAT
I'M GOING SNOWBOARDING THIS WEEKEND!
BUS STOP
WHERE ARE YOU STAYING?
A CABIN ON SNOWY MOUNTAIN.
A CABIN? EVERYBODY KNOWS THE PLACE TO STAY IS THE CHALET HOTEL.
IT HAS A HOT TUB.
POP!
SIGH.
SSSSSS
FEELING A LITTLE DEFLATED, BABYMOUSE?

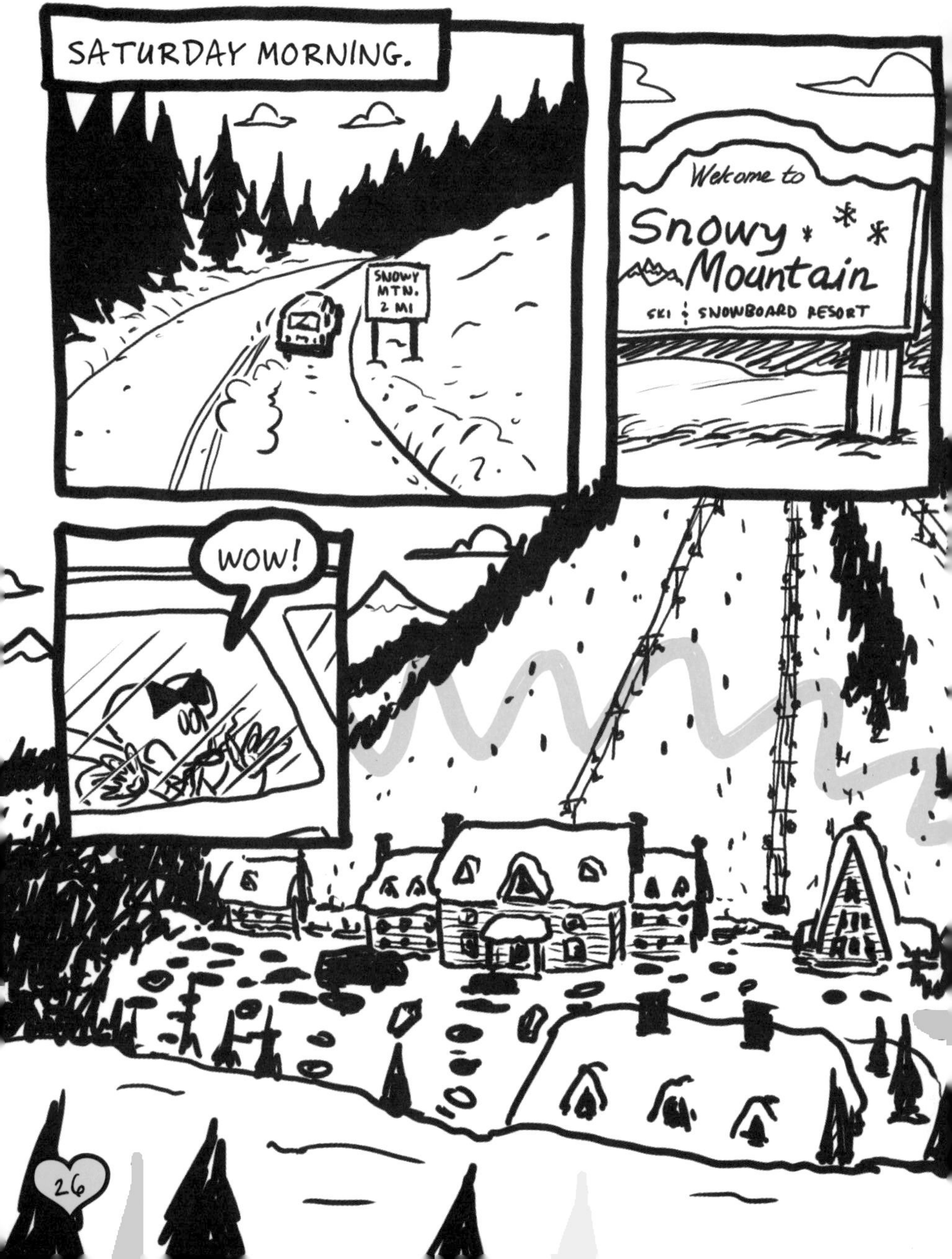
SATURDAY MORNING.
SNOWY MTN. 2 MI
Welcome to Snowy Mountain
SKI & SNOWBOARD RESORT
WOW!

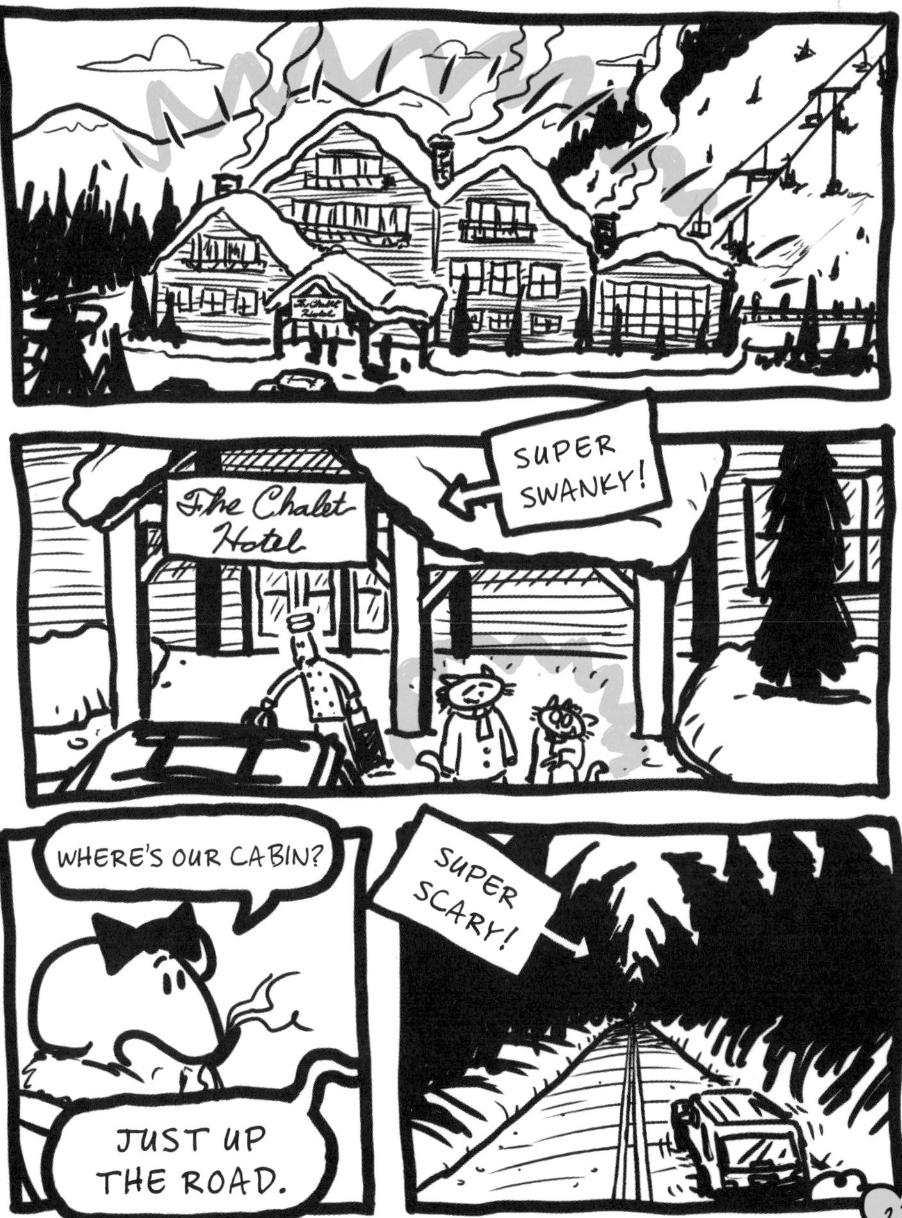
The Chalet Hotel
SUPER SWANKY!
The Chalet Hotel
WHERE'S OUR CABIN?
JUST UP THE ROAD.
SUPER SCARY!

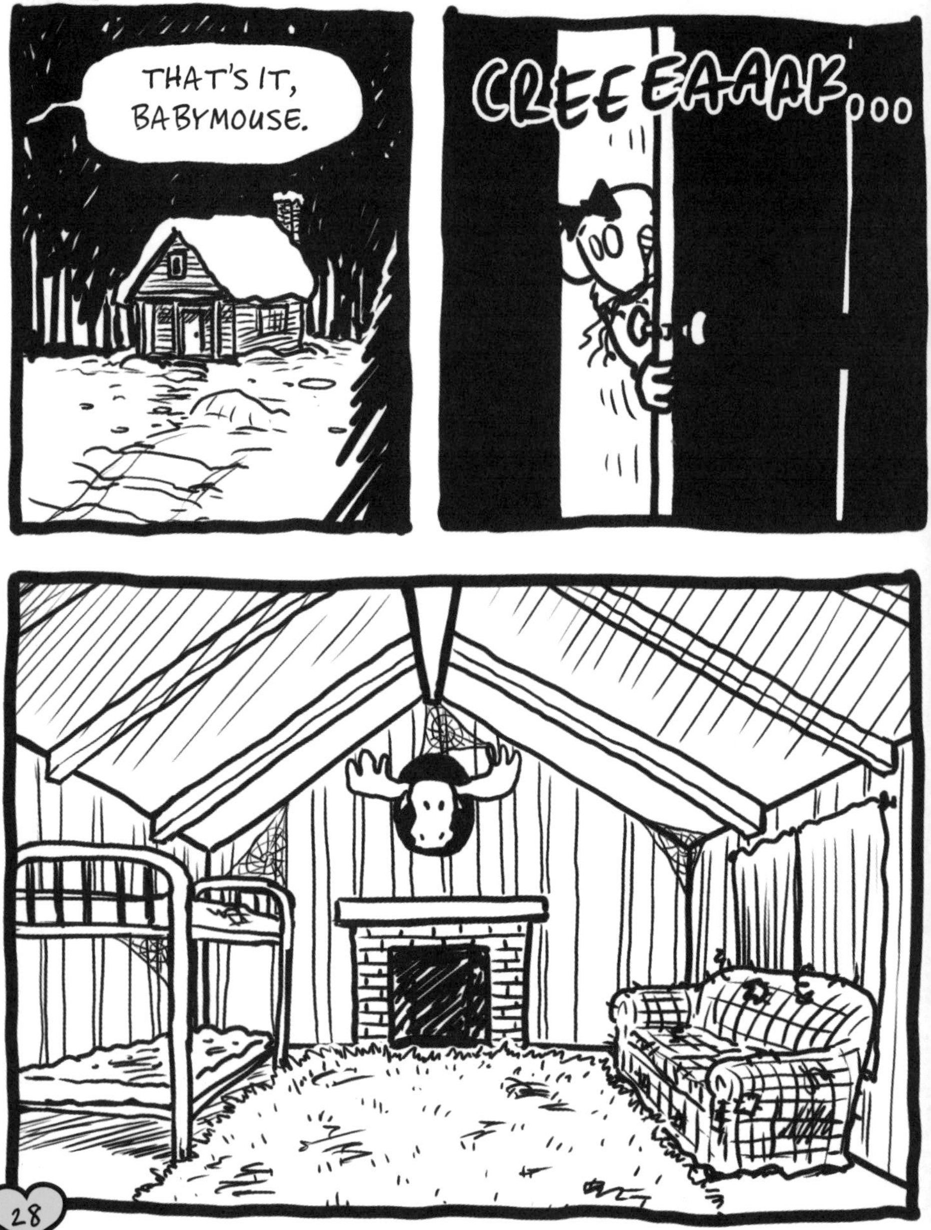
THAT'S IT, BABYMOUSE.
CREEEAAAK...

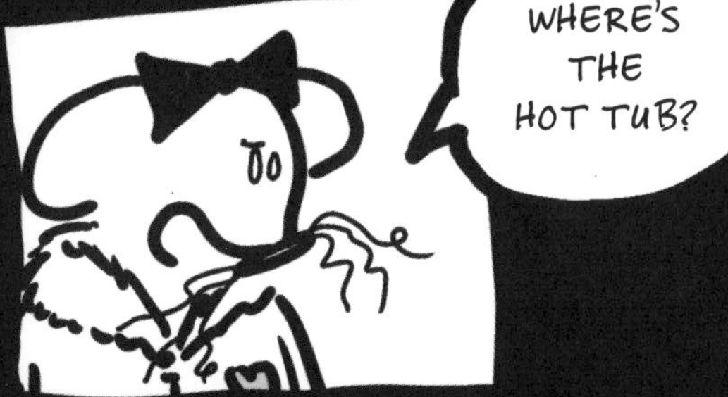
WHERE'S THE HOT TUB?

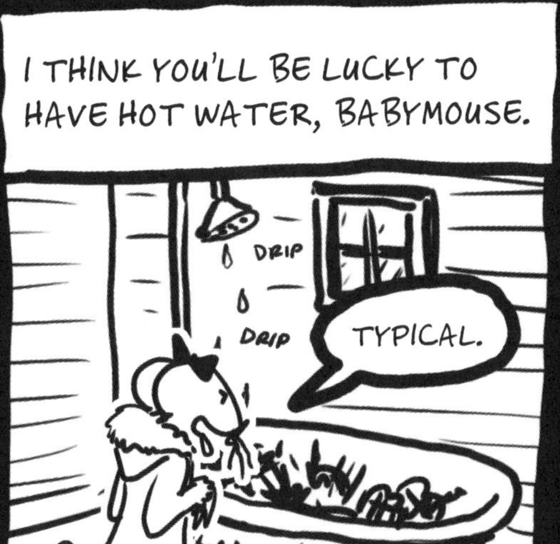
I THINK YOU'LL BE LUCKY TO HAVE HOT WATER, BABYMOUSE.
DRIP
DRIP
TYPICAL.

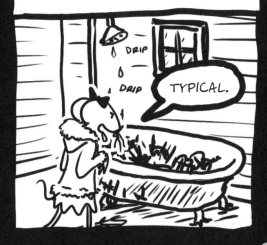

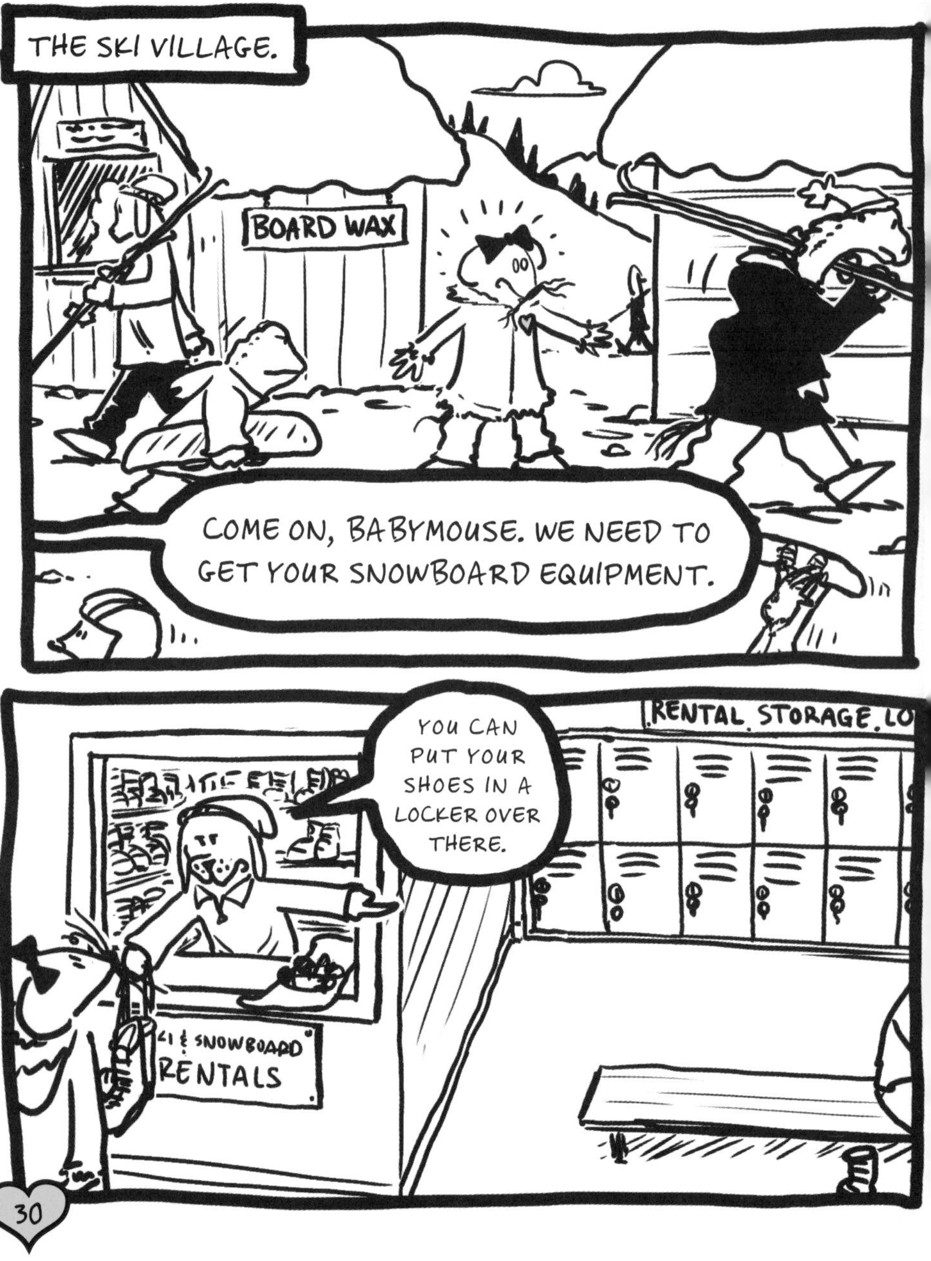
THE SKI VILLAGE.
BOARD WAX
COME ON, BABYMOUSE. WE NEED TO GET YOUR SNOWBOARD EQUIPMENT.
RENTAL STORAGE
YOU CAN PUT YOUR SHOES IN A LOCKER OVER THERE.
& SNOWBOARD
RENTALS

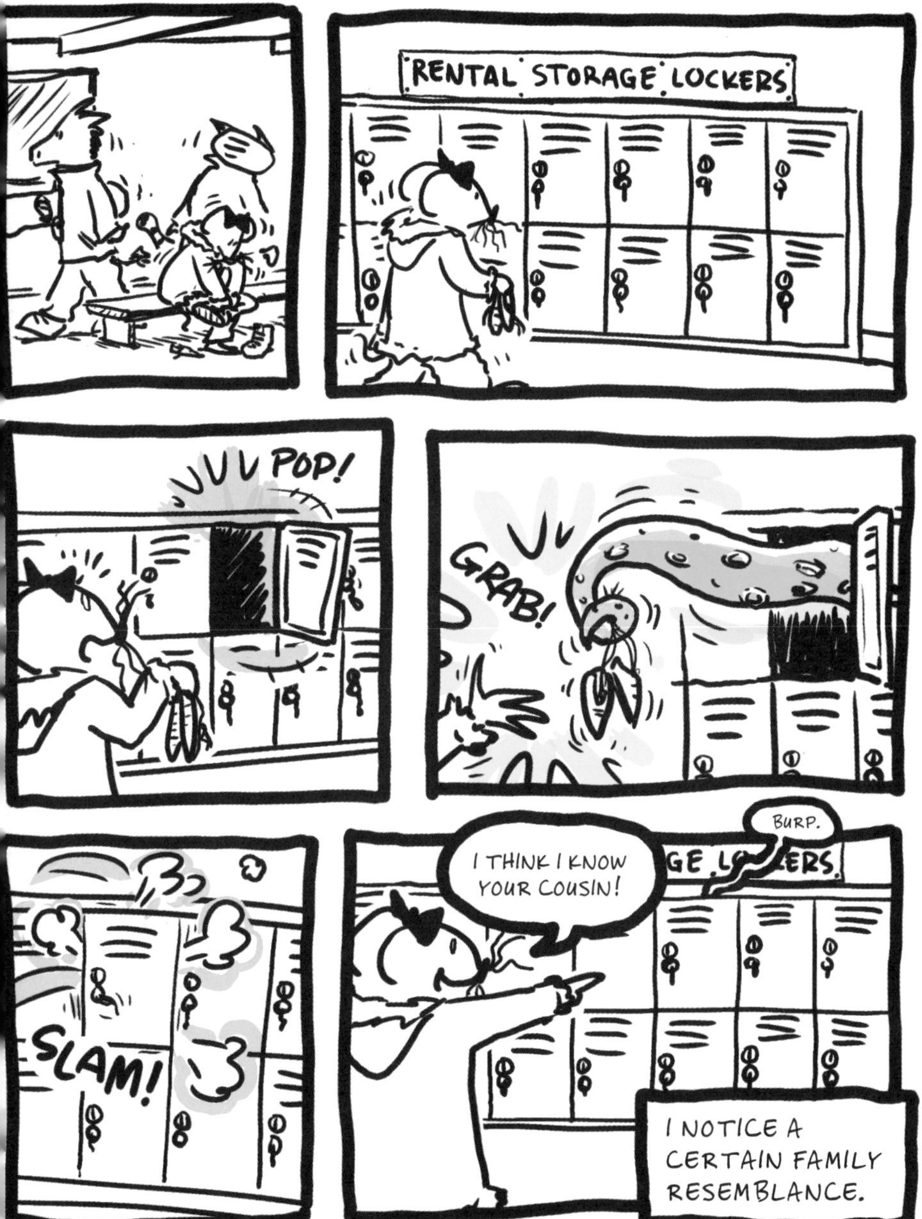
RENTAL STORAGE LOCKERS
POP!
GRAB!
SLAM!
I THINK I KNOW YOUR COUSIN!
BURP.
I NOTICE A CERTAIN FAMILY RESEMBLANCE.

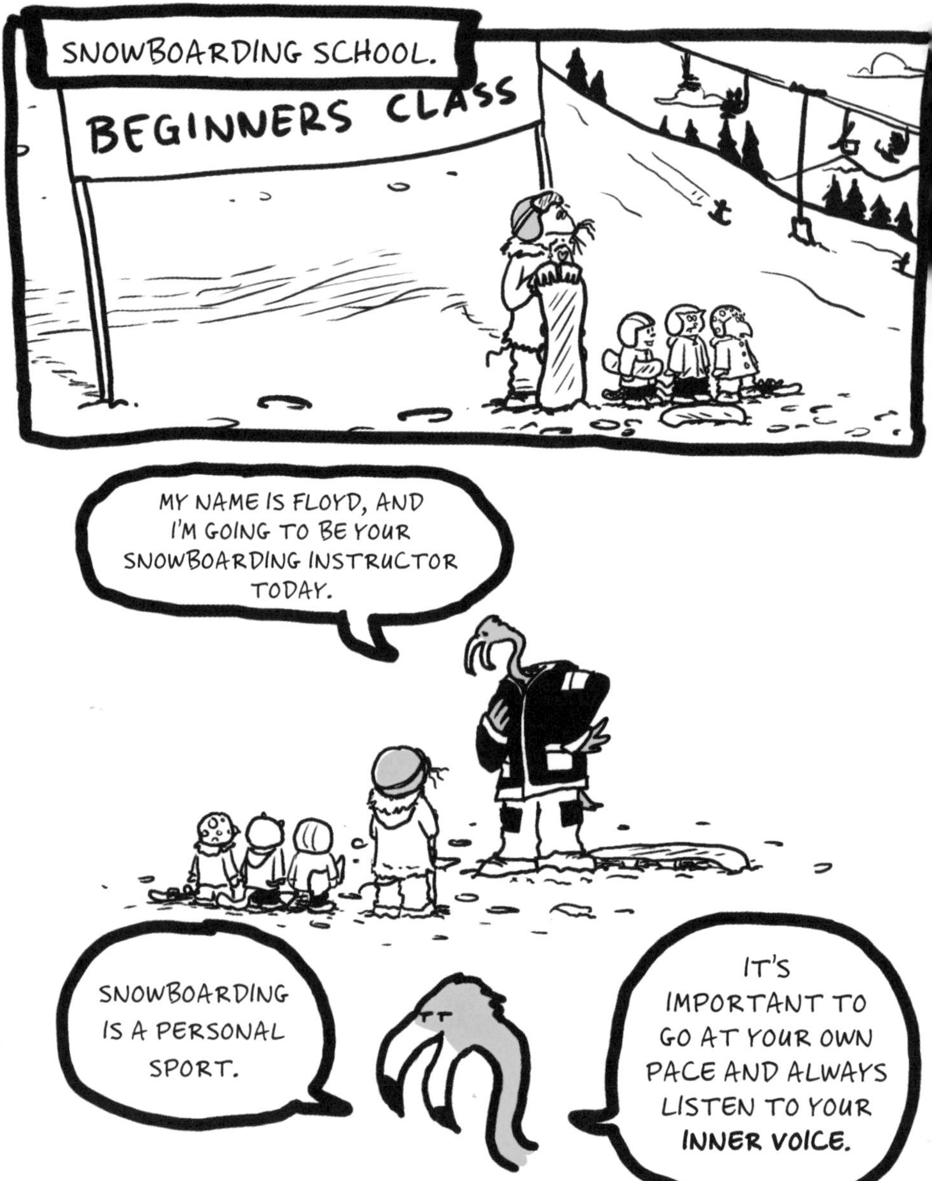
SNOWBOARDING SCHOOL.
BEGINNERS CLASS
MY NAME IS FLOYD, AND I'M GOING TO BE YOUR SNOWBOARDING INSTRUCTOR TODAY.
SNOWBOARDING IS A PERSONAL SPORT.
IT'S IMPORTANT TO GO AT YOUR OWN PACE AND ALWAYS LISTEN TO YOUR **INNER VOICE.**

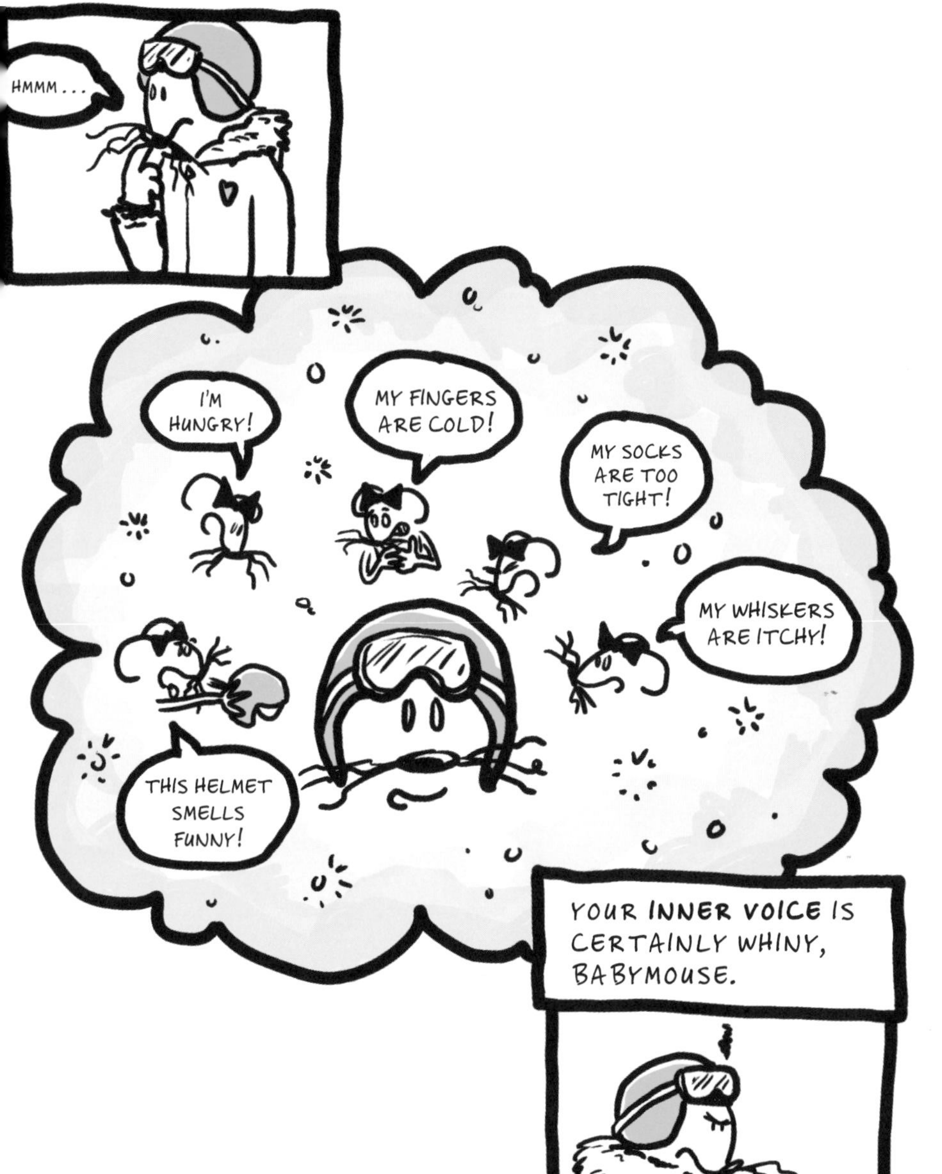
HMMM...
I'M HUNGRY!
MY FINGERS ARE COLD!
MY SOCKS ARE TOO TIGHT!
MY WHISKERS ARE ITCHY!
THIS HELMET SMELLS FUNNY!
YOUR INNER VOICE IS CERTAINLY WHINY, BABYMOUSE.

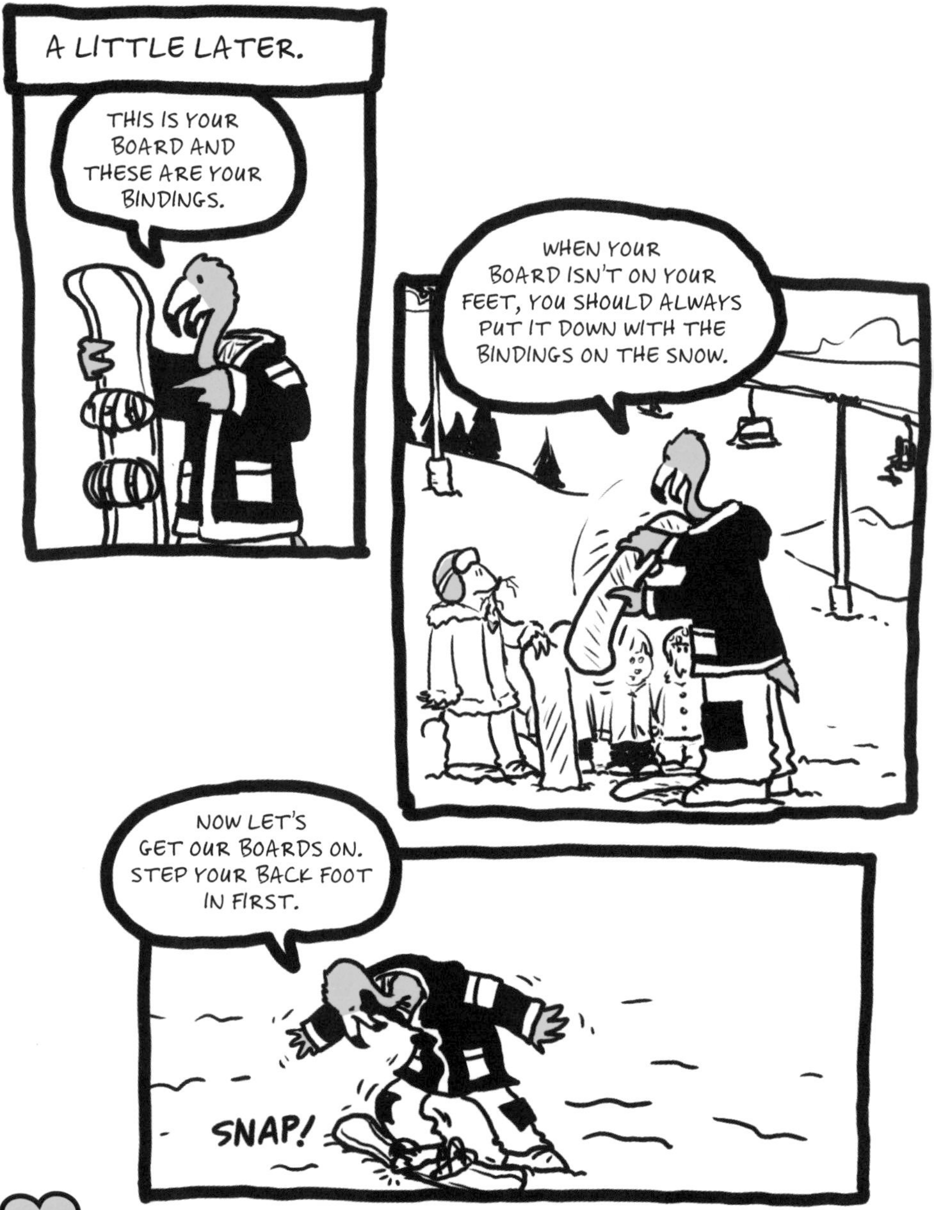
A LITTLE LATER.
THIS IS YOUR BOARD AND THESE ARE YOUR BINDINGS.
WHEN YOUR BOARD ISN'T ON YOUR FEET, YOU SHOULD ALWAYS PUT IT DOWN WITH THE BINDINGS ON THE SNOW.
NOW LET'S GET OUR BOARDS ON. STEP YOUR BACK FOOT IN FIRST.
SNAP!

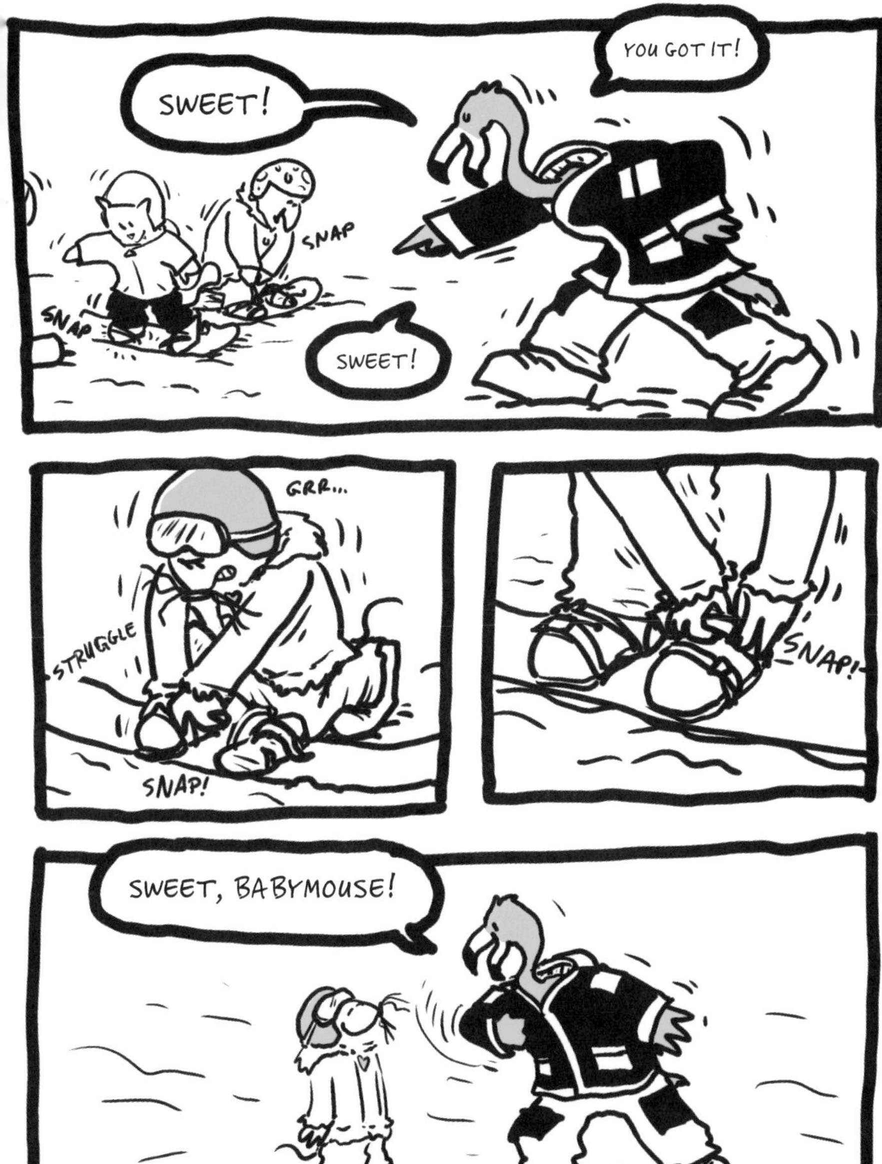
SWEET!
YOU GOT IT!
SNAP
SNAP
SWEET!
GRR...
STRUGGLE
SNAP!
SNAP!
SWEET, BABYMOUSE!

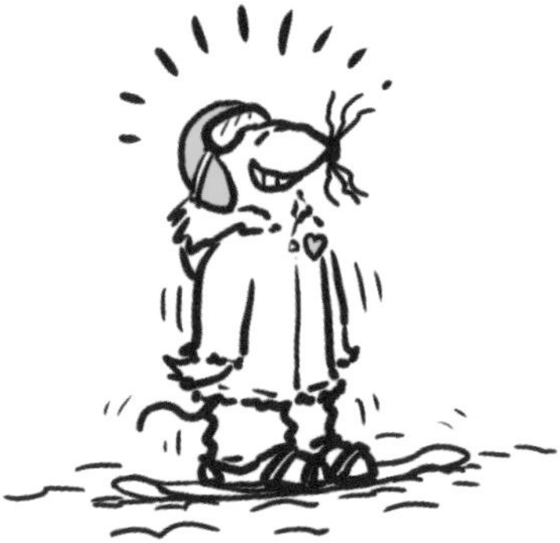

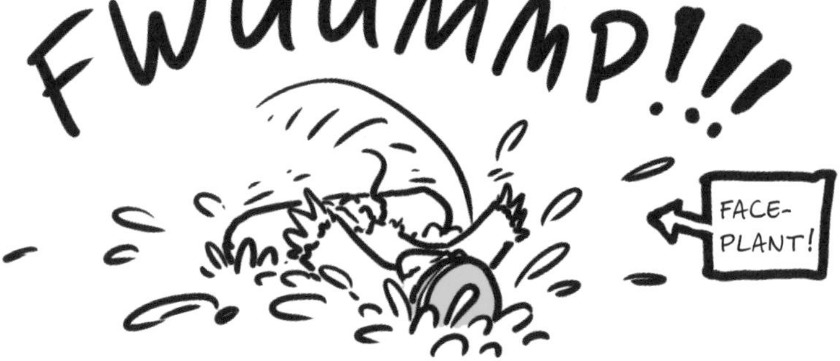
FWUUMMP!!!
FACE-PLANT!

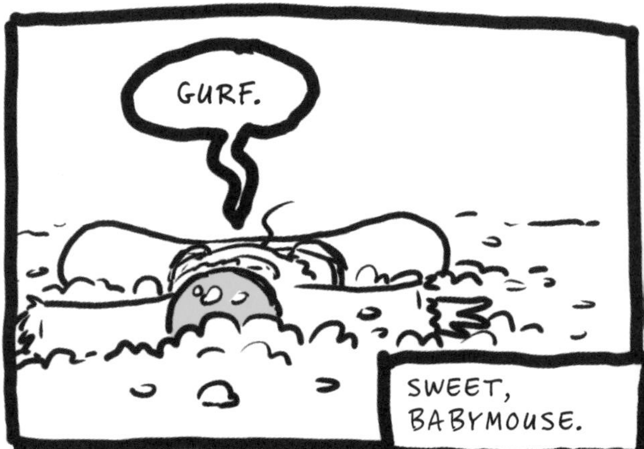
GURF.
SWEET, BABYMOUSE.

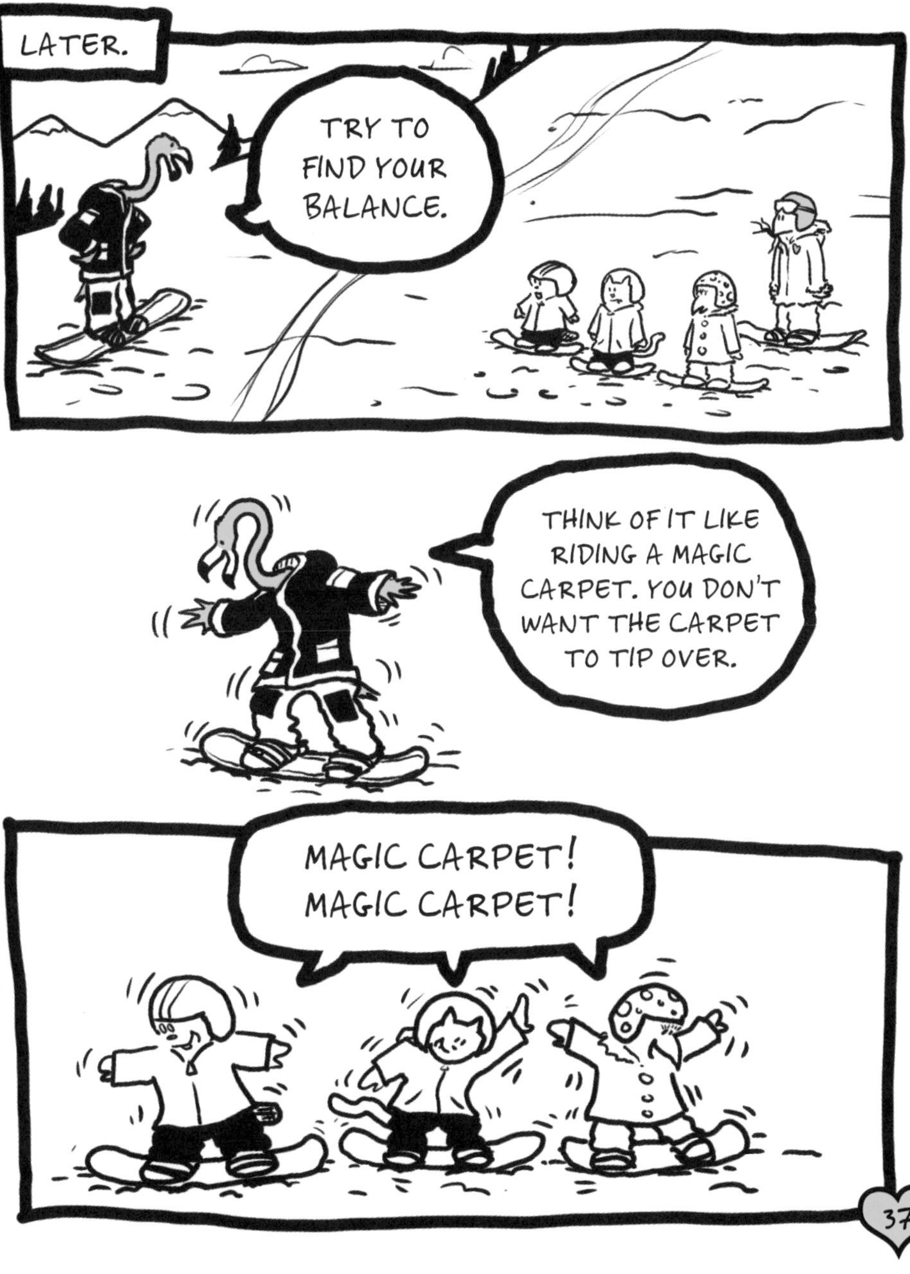
LATER.
TRY TO FIND YOUR BALANCE.
THINK OF IT LIKE RIDING A MAGIC CARPET. YOU DON'T WANT THE CARPET TO TIP OVER.
MAGIC CARPET! MAGIC CARPET!

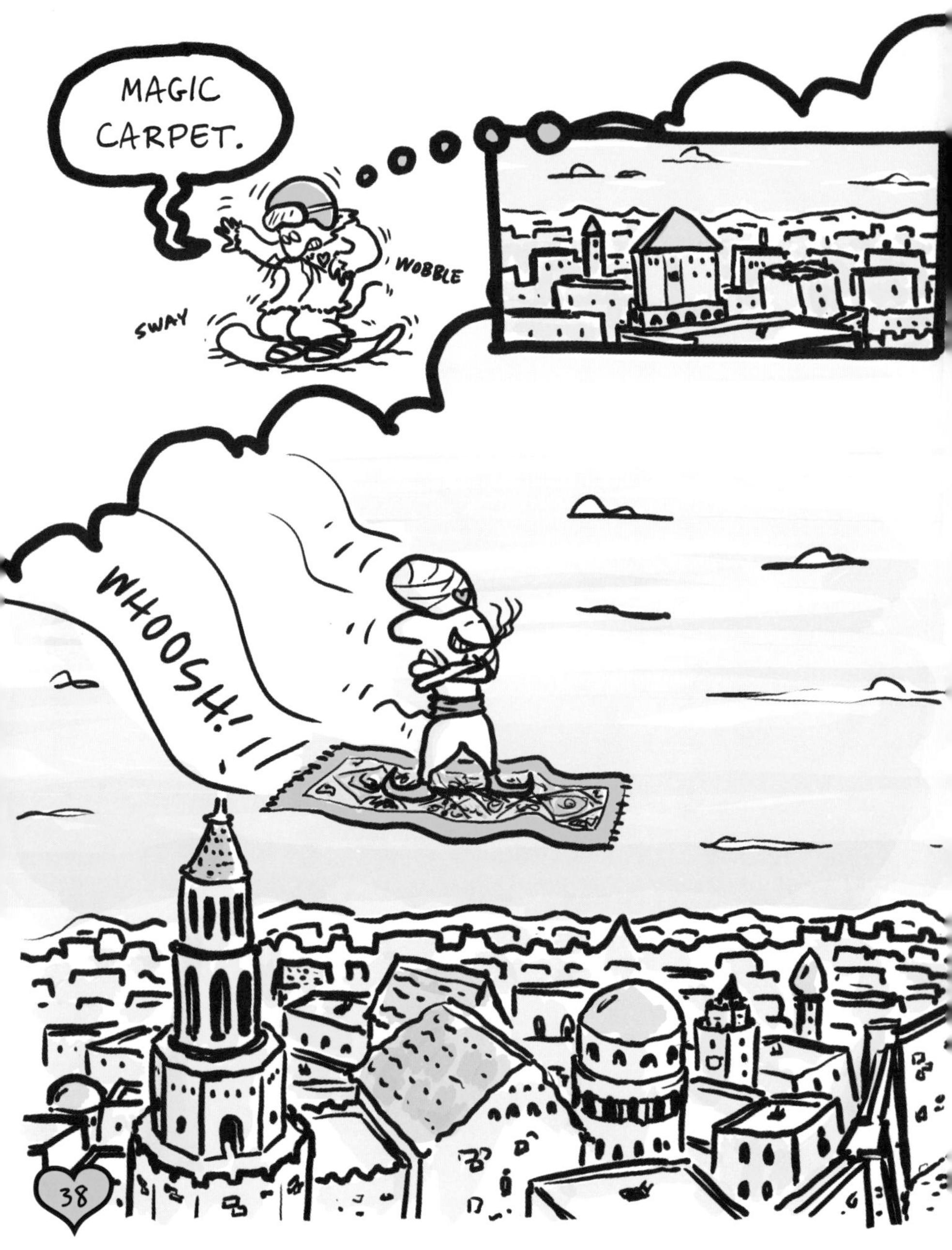
MAGIC CARPET.
WOBBLE
SWAY
WHOOSH!

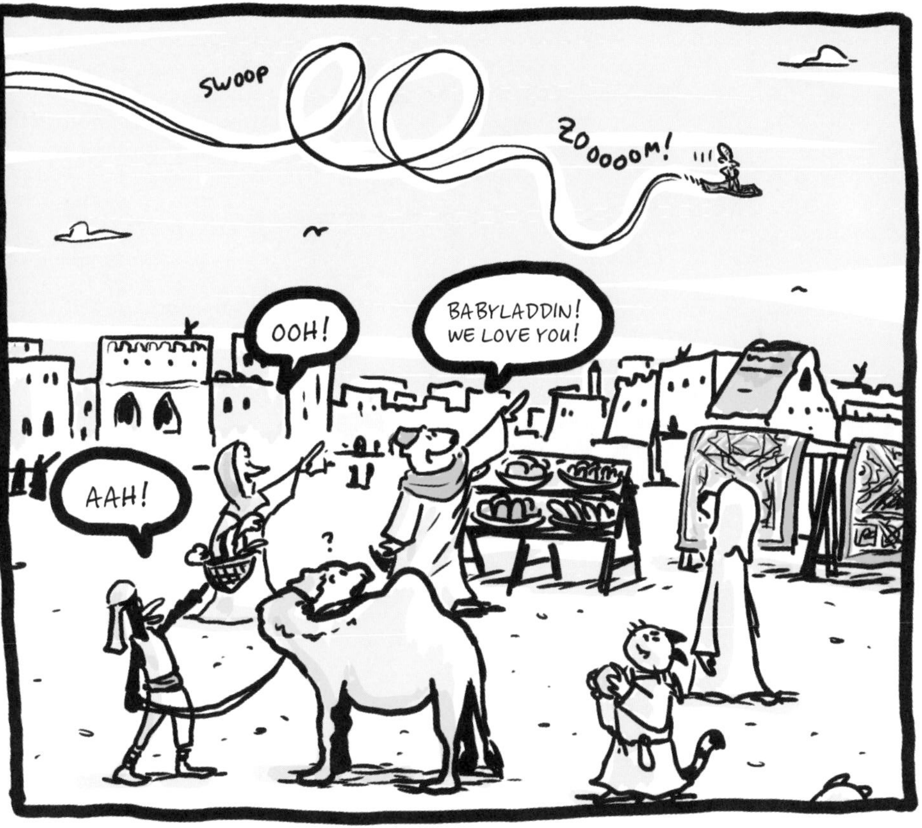
SWOOP
ZOOOOOM!
OOH!
BABYLADDIN! WE LOVE YOU!
AAH!
?

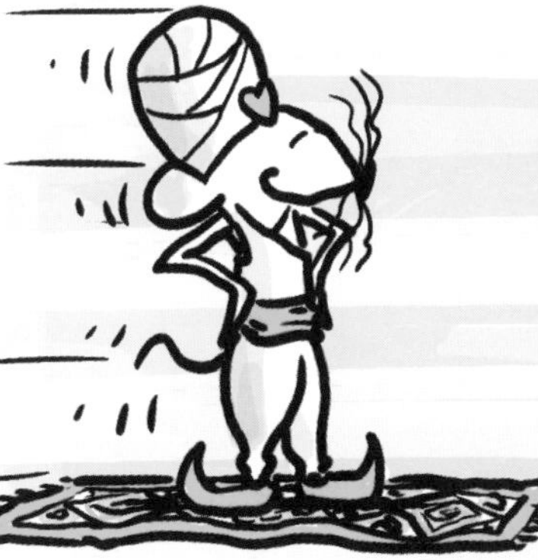

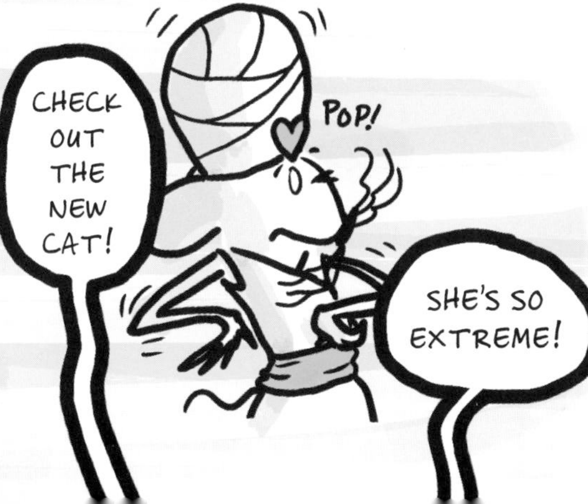
CHECK OUT THE NEW CAT!
POP!
SHE'S SO EXTREME!

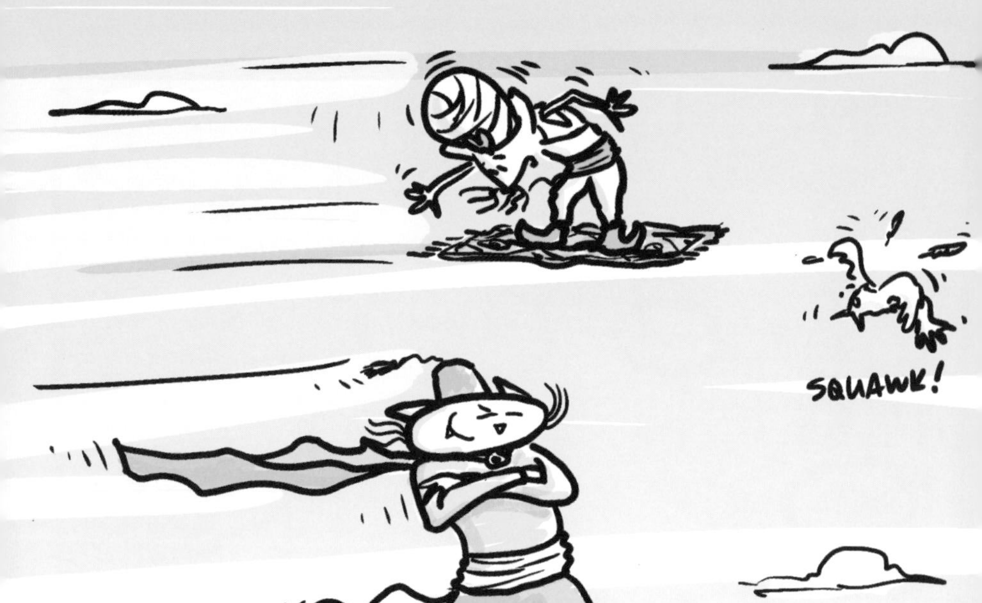
SQUAWK!

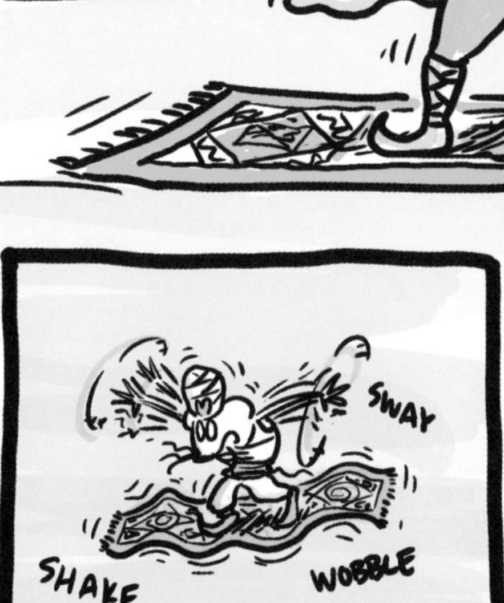
SWAY
SHAKE
WOBBLE

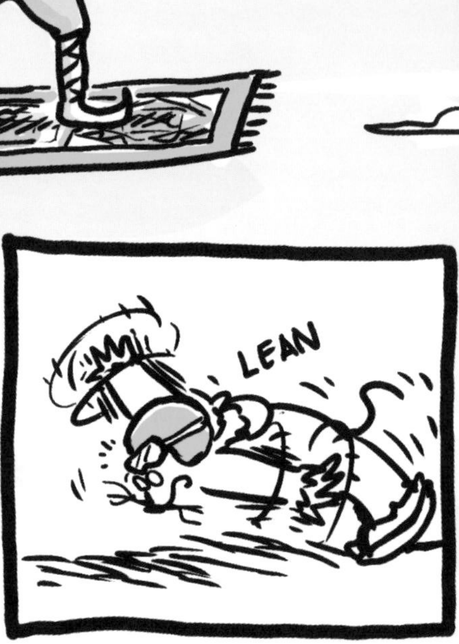
LEAN

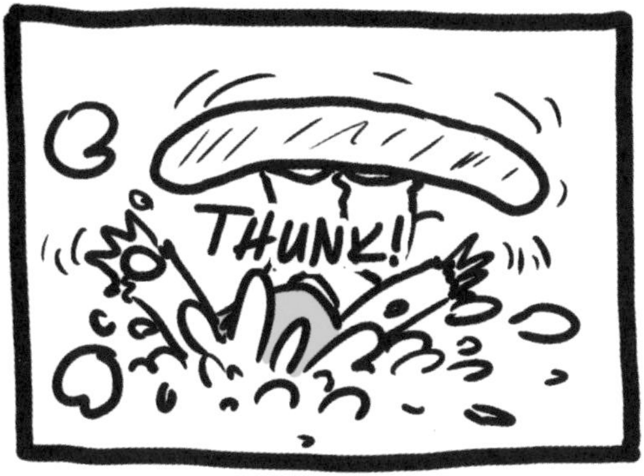
THUNK!

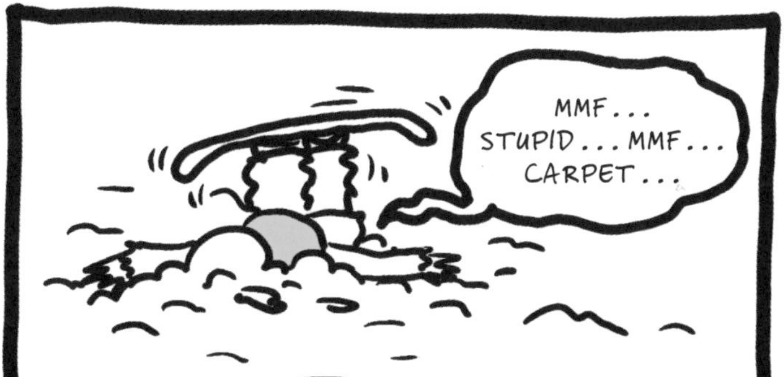
MMF . . .
STUPID . . . MMF . . .
CARPET . . .

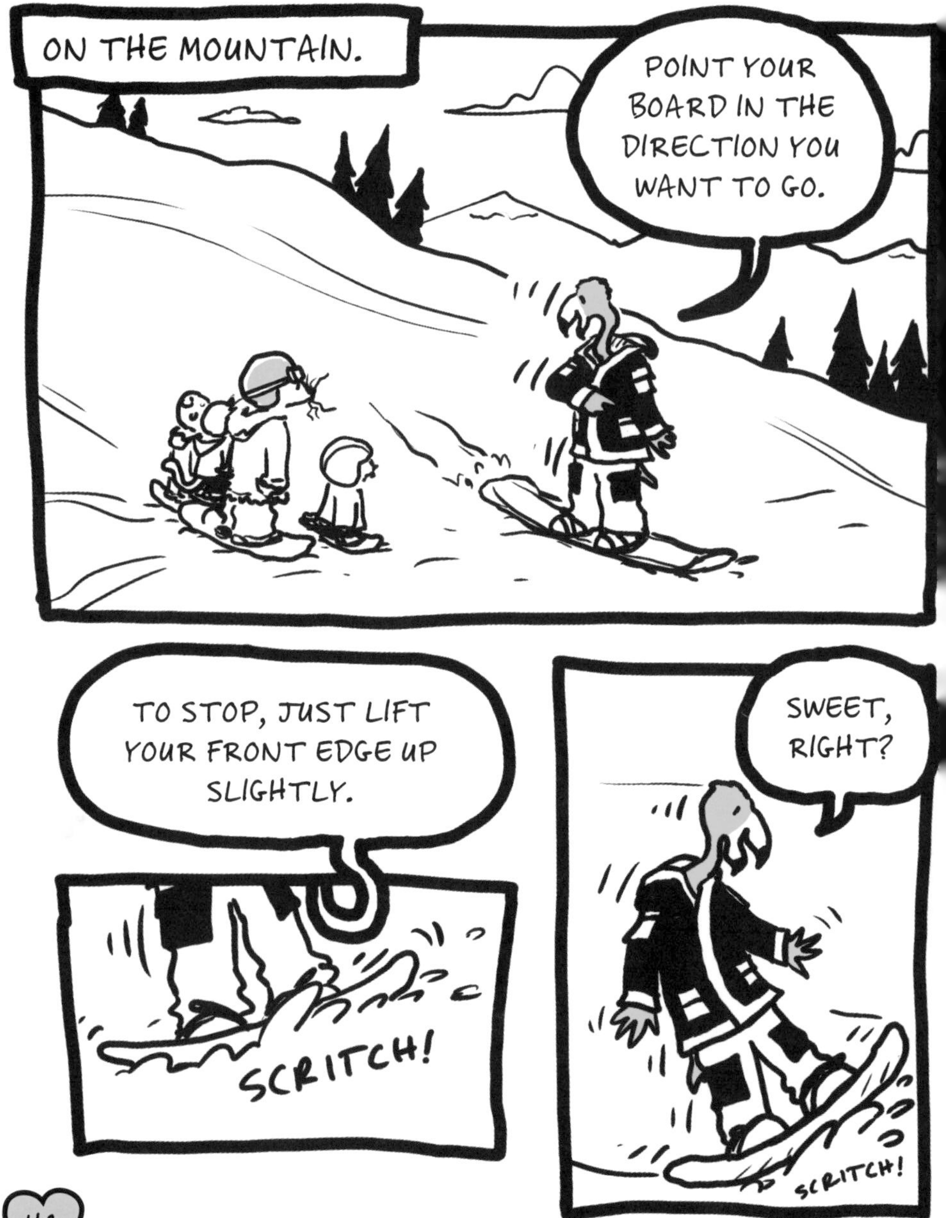
ON THE MOUNTAIN.
POINT YOUR BOARD IN THE DIRECTION YOU WANT TO GO.
TO STOP, JUST LIFT YOUR FRONT EDGE UP SLIGHTLY.
SCRITCH!
SWEET, RIGHT?
SCRITCH!

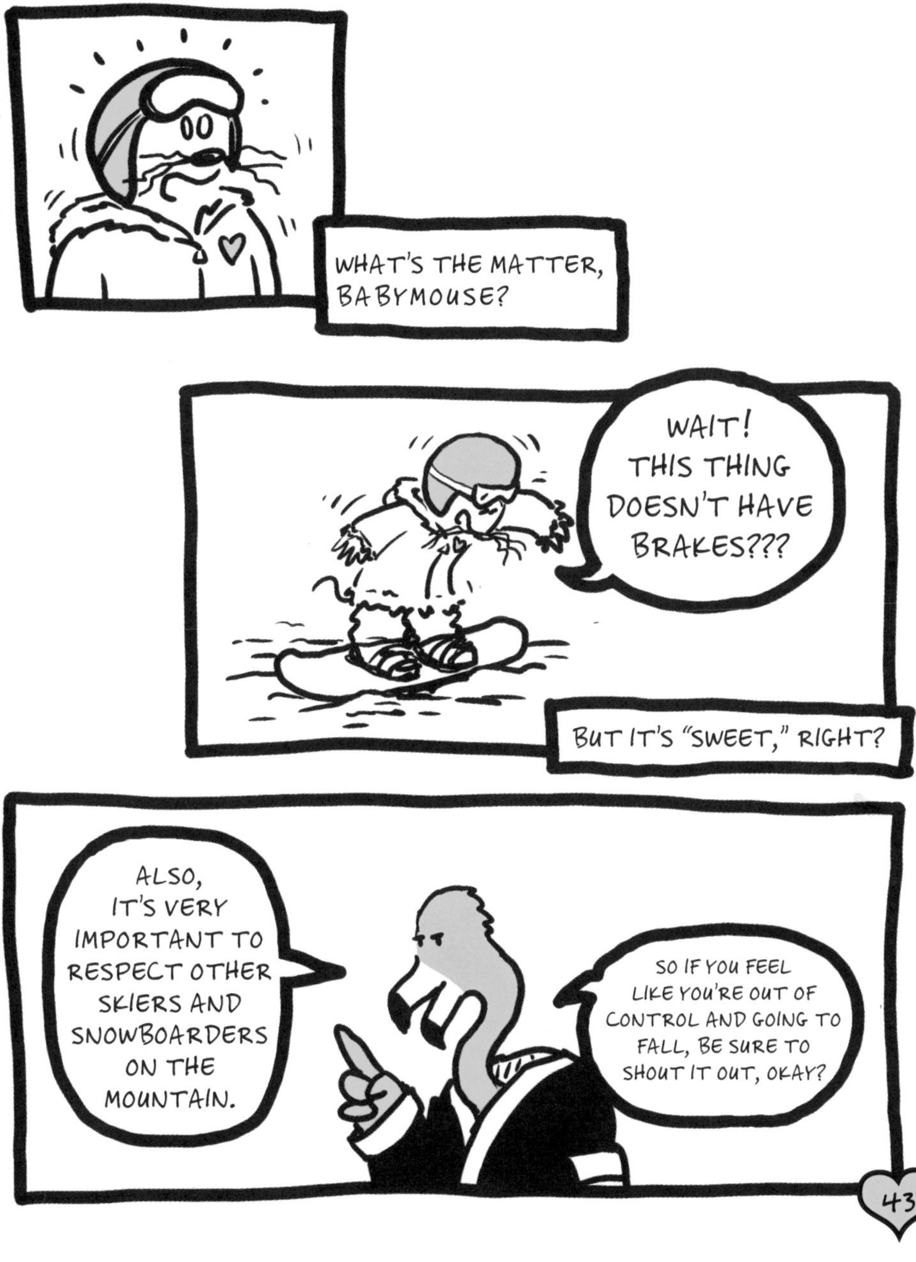
WHAT'S THE MATTER, BABYMOUSE?
WAIT! THIS THING DOESN'T HAVE BRAKES???
BUT IT'S "SWEET," RIGHT?
ALSO, IT'S VERY IMPORTANT TO RESPECT OTHER SKIERS AND SNOWBOARDERS ON THE MOUNTAIN.
SO IF YOU FEEL LIKE YOU'RE OUT OF CONTROL AND GOING TO FALL, BE SURE TO SHOUT IT OUT, OKAY?

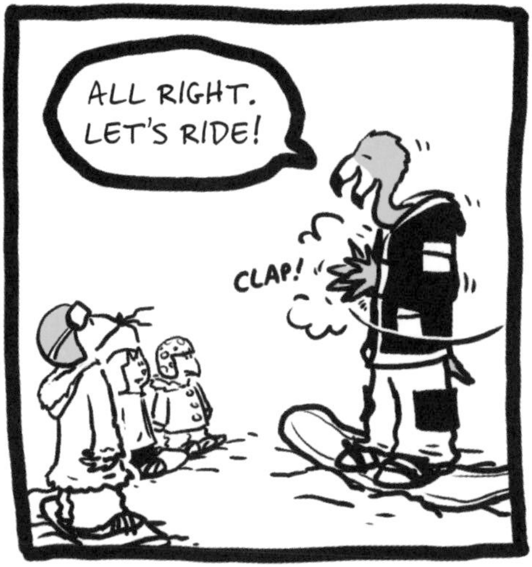
ALL RIGHT.
LET'S RIDE!
CLAP!

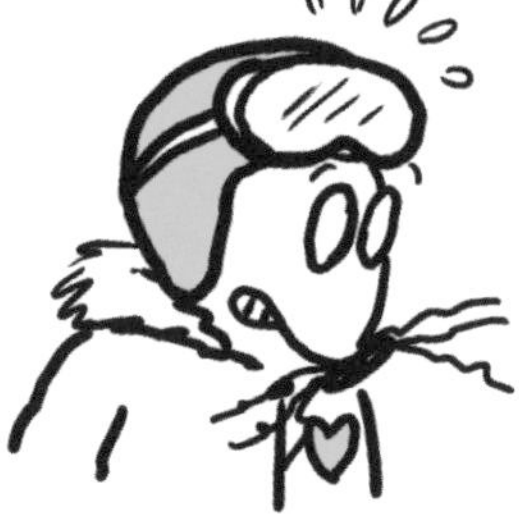

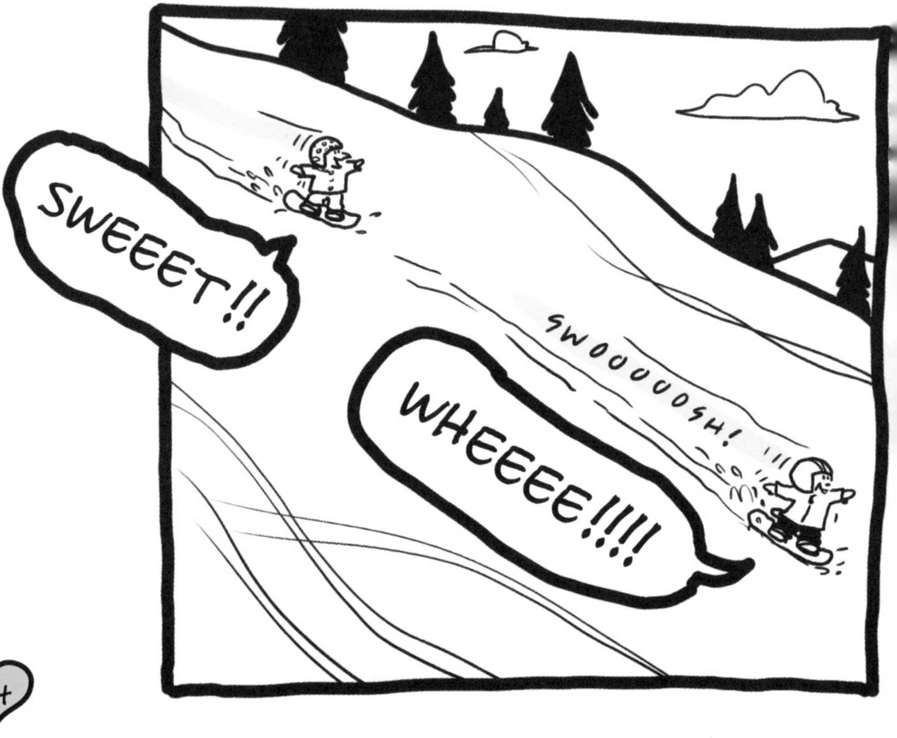
SWEEEET!!
SWOOOOOOSH!
WHEEEEE!!!!

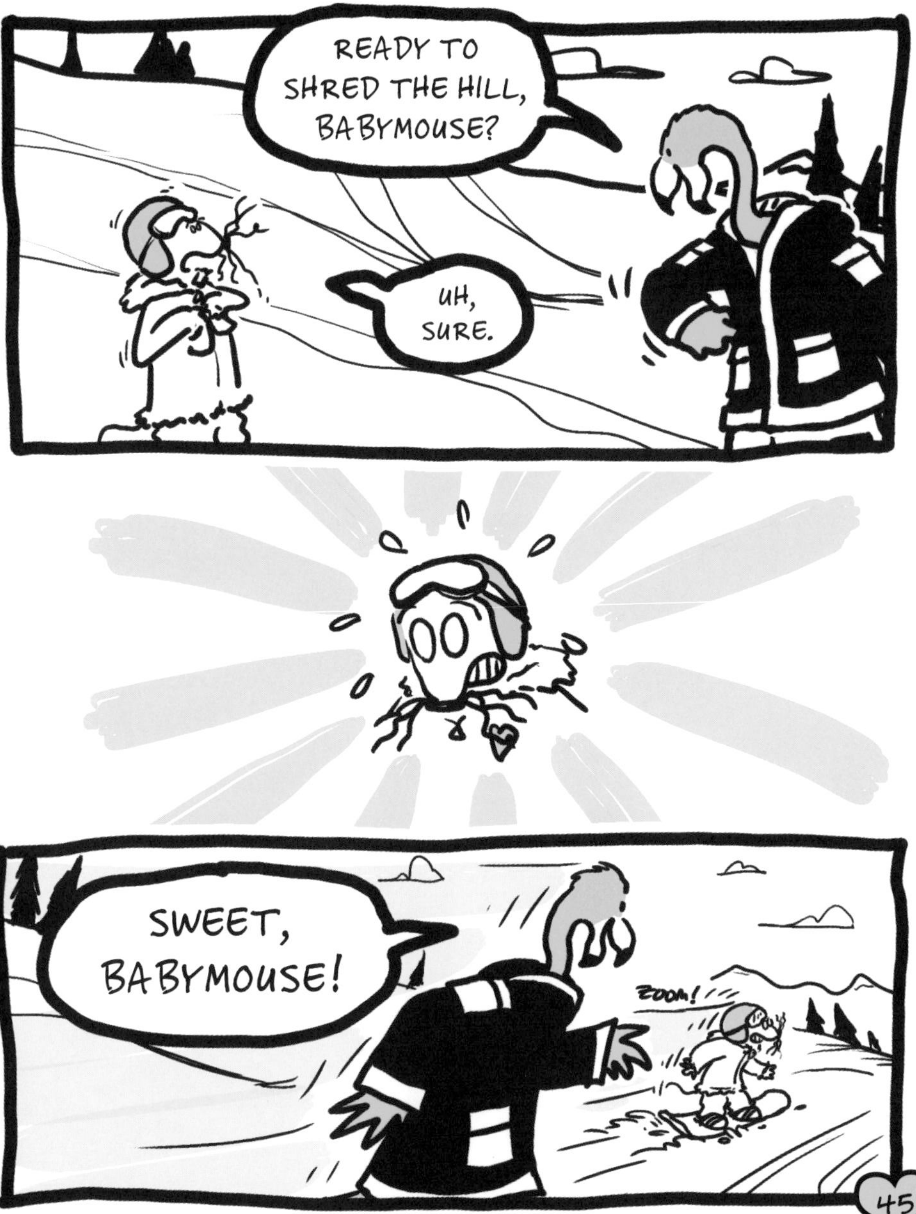
READY TO SHRED THE HILL, BABYMOUSE?
UH, SURE.
SWEET, BABYMOUSE!
ZOOM!

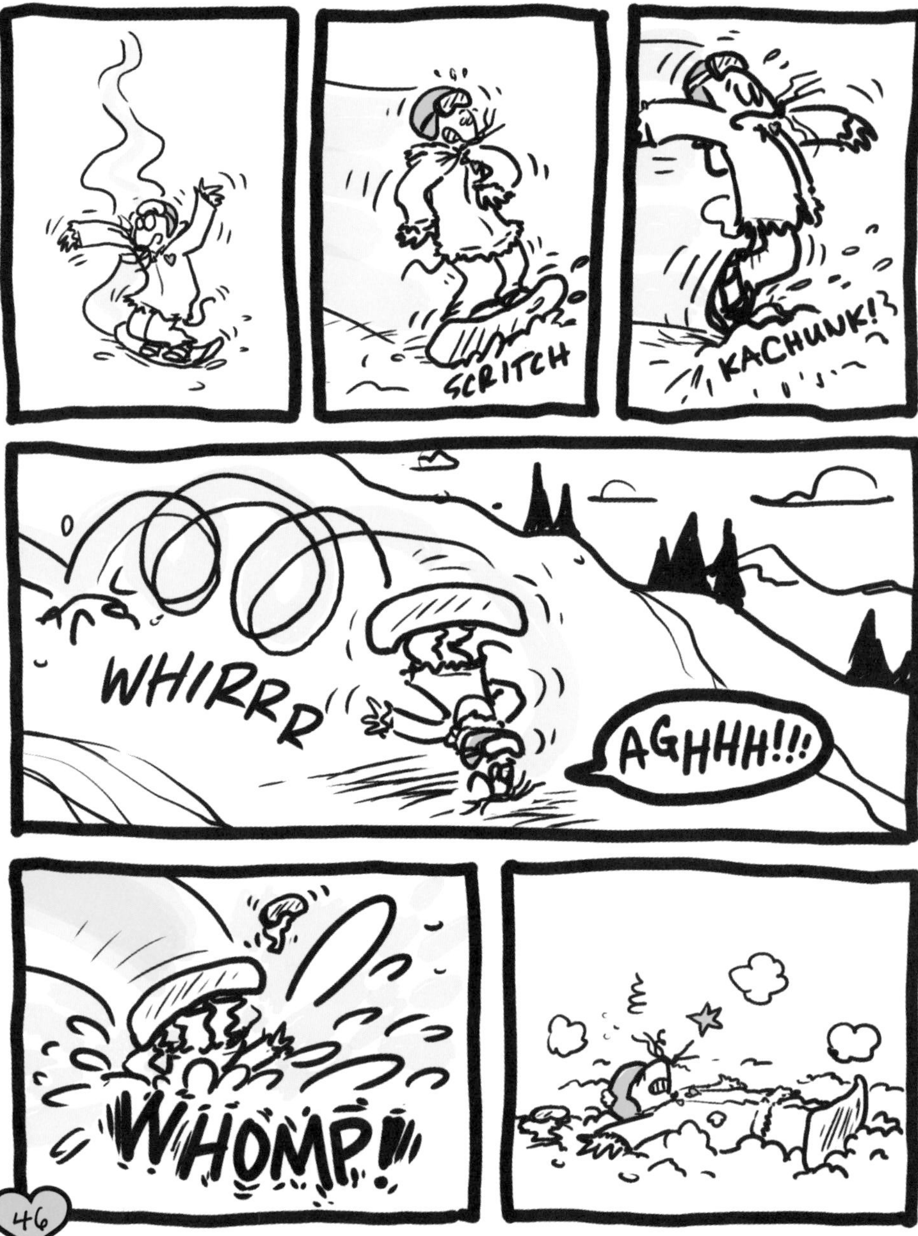
SCRITCH
KACHUNK!
WHIRRRR
AGHHH!!!
WHOMP!

DID YOU FORGET SOMETHING, BABYMOUSE?
OH, YEAH.
"I'M FALLING."

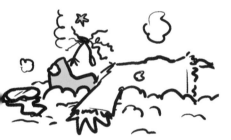

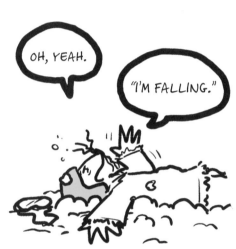

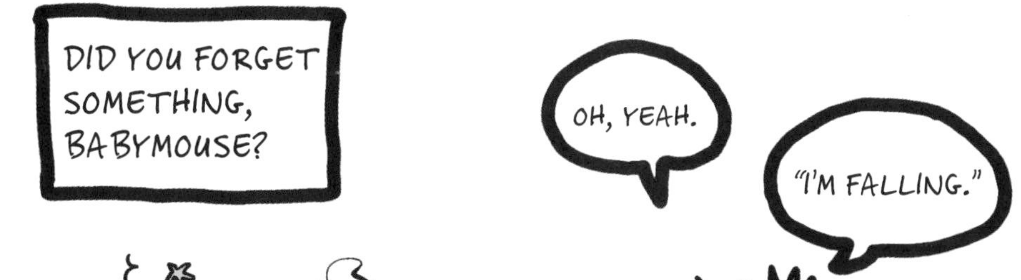

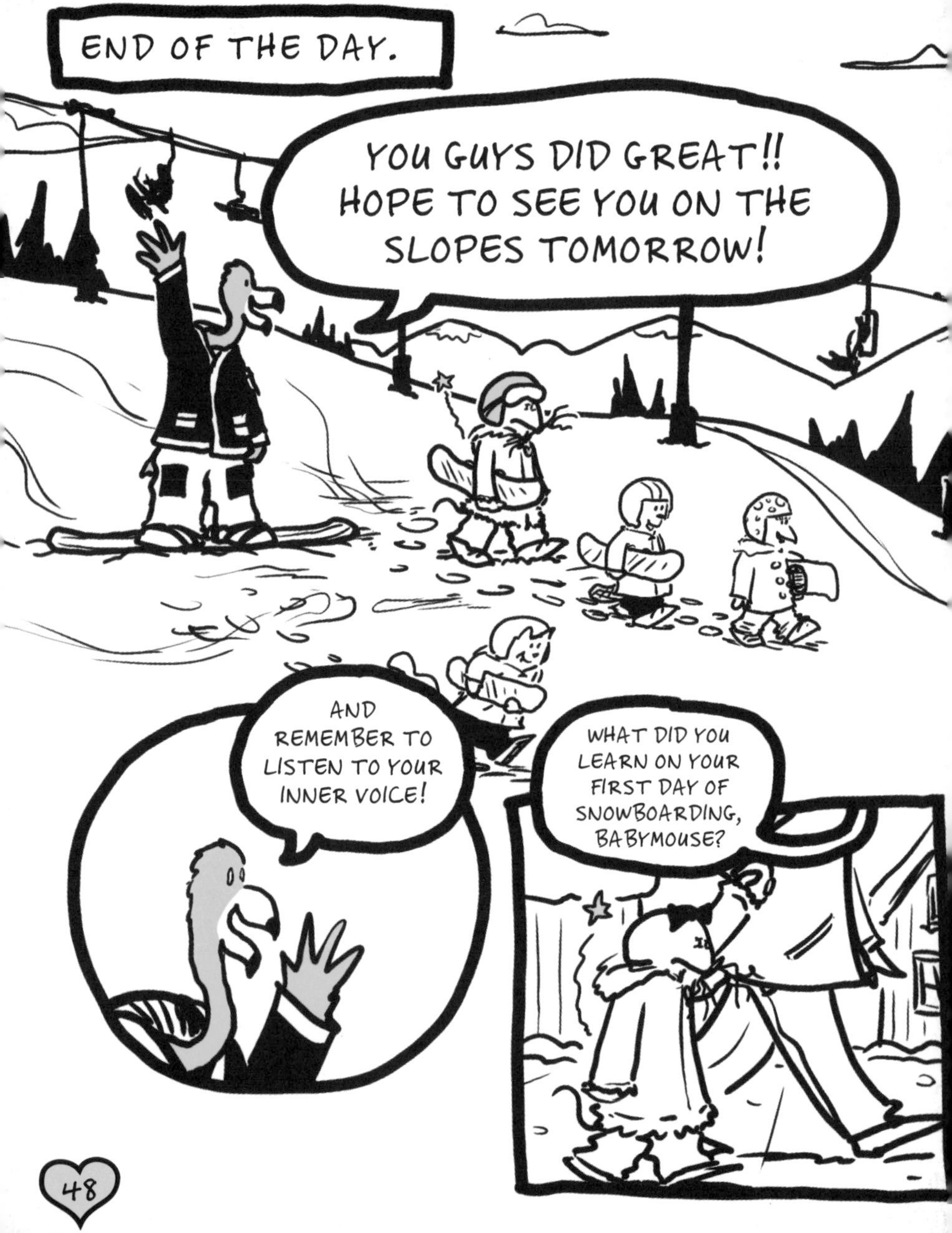

END OF THE DAY.
YOU GUYS DID GREAT!! HOPE TO SEE YOU ON THE SLOPES TOMORROW!
AND REMEMBER TO LISTEN TO YOUR INNER VOICE!
WHAT DID YOU LEARN ON YOUR FIRST DAY OF SNOWBOARDING, BABYMOUSE?

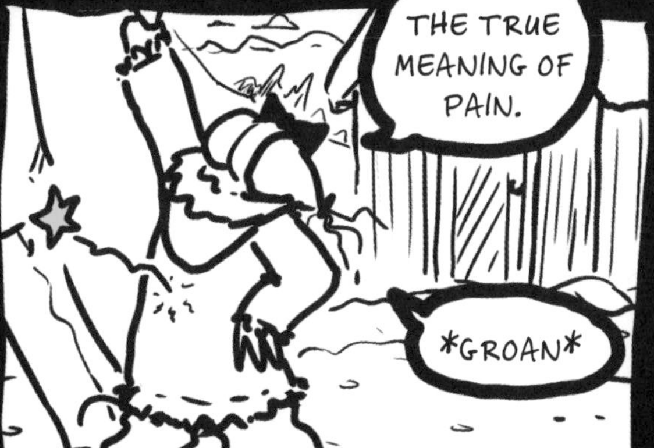
THE TRUE MEANING OF PAIN.
GROAN

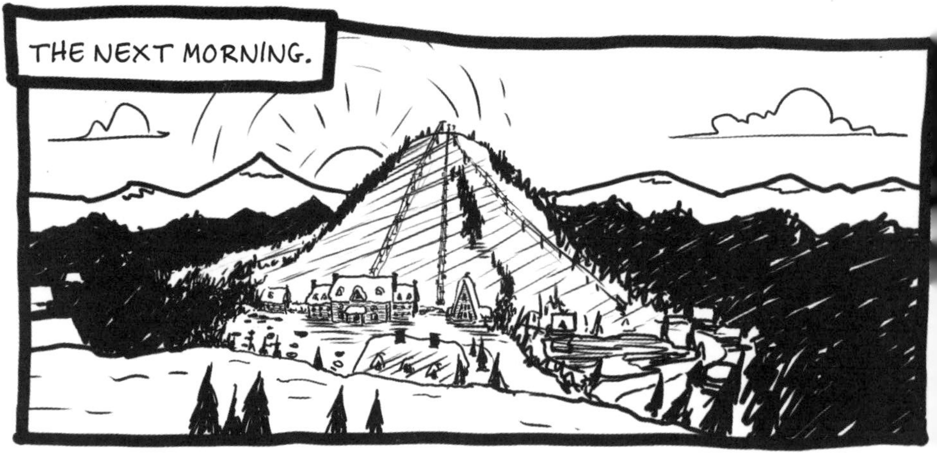
THE NEXT MORNING.

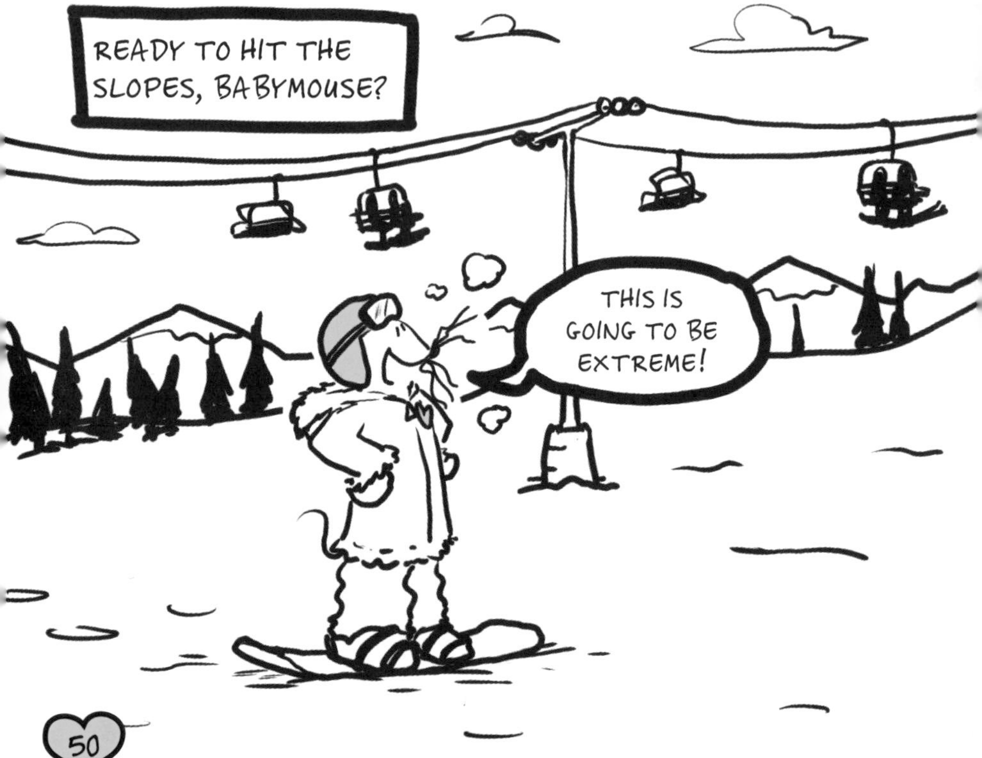
READY TO HIT THE SLOPES, BABYMOUSE?
THIS IS GOING TO BE EXTREME!

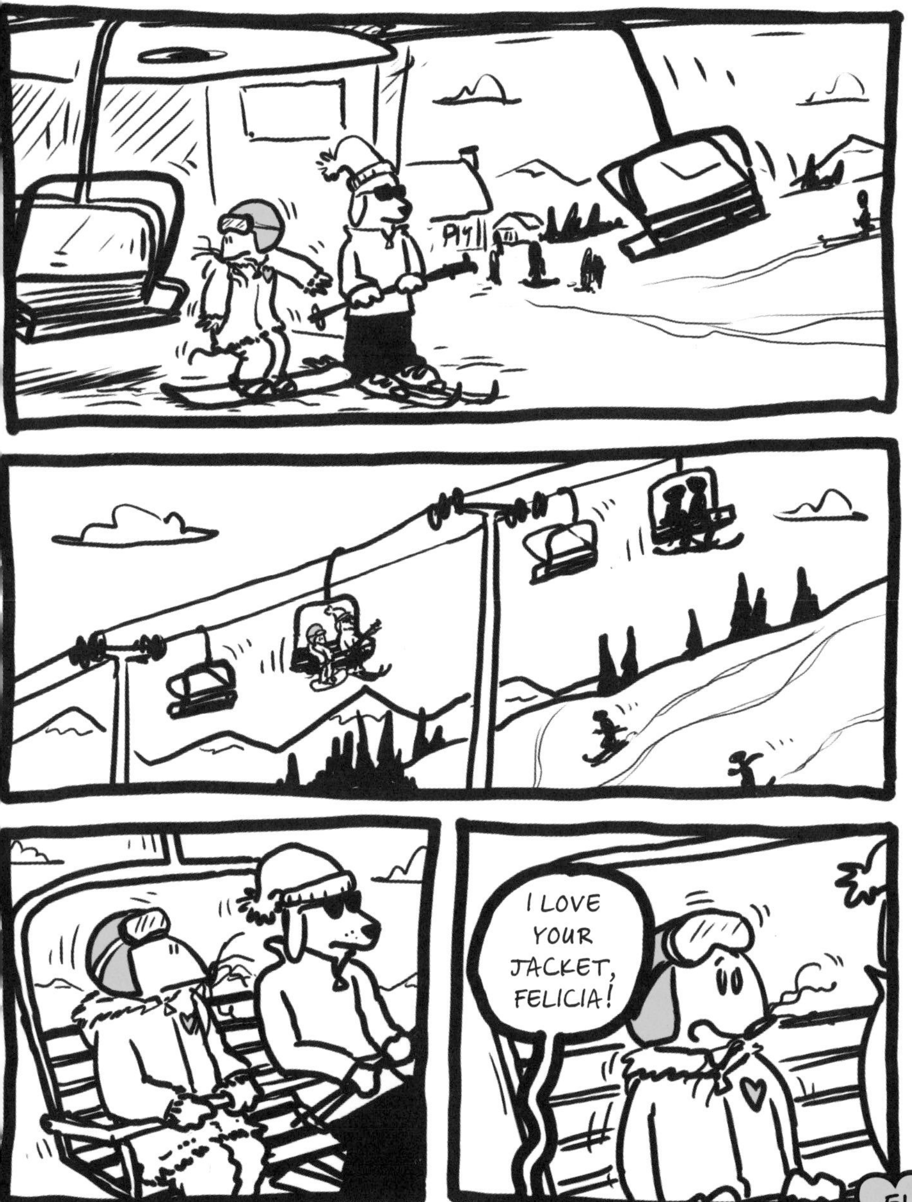

P14
I LOVE YOUR JACKET, FELICIA!

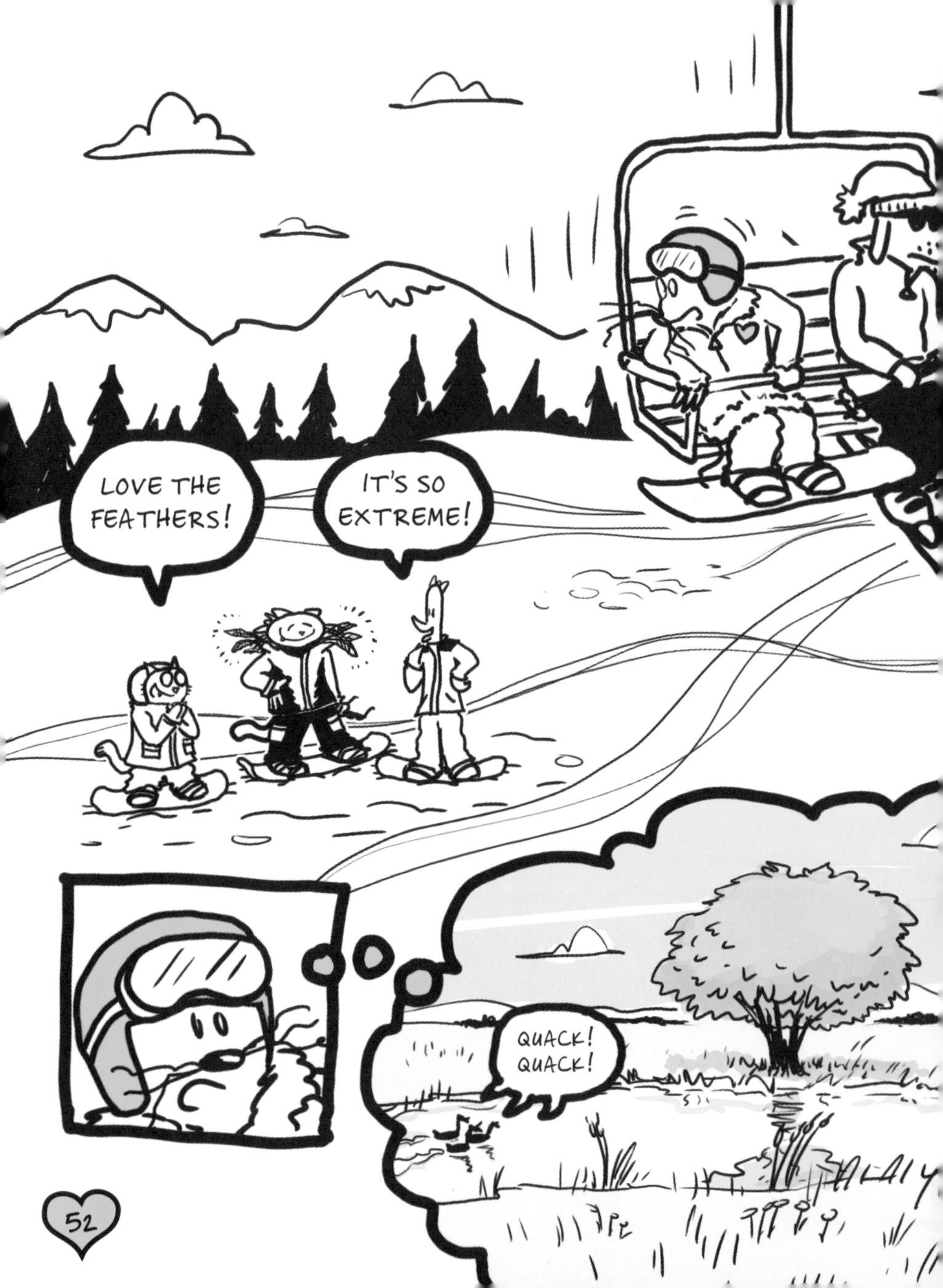
LOVE THE FEATHERS!
IT'S SO EXTREME!
QUACK! QUACK!

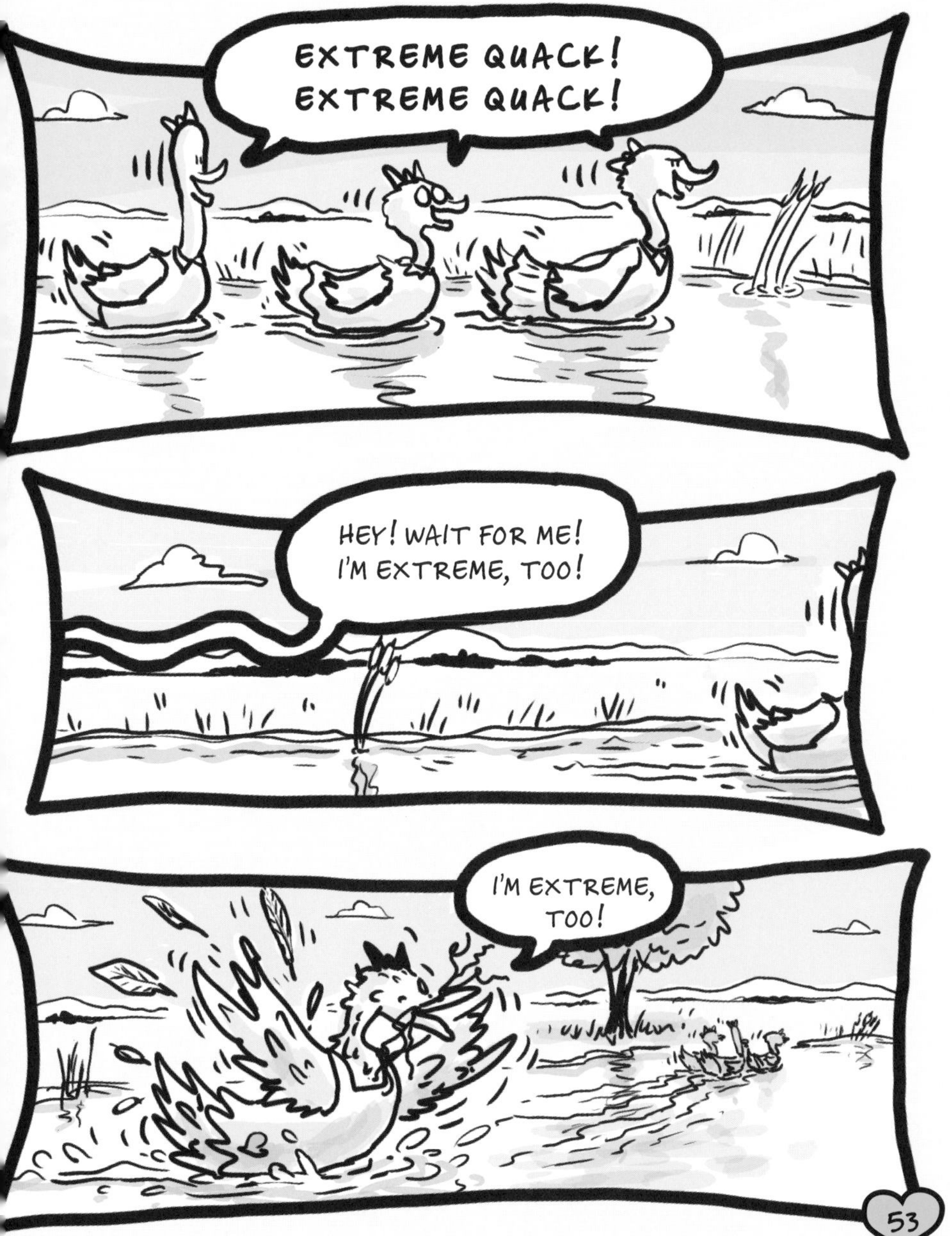
EXTREME QUACK!
EXTREME QUACK!
HEY! WAIT FOR ME!
I'M EXTREME, TOO!
I'M EXTREME,
TOO!

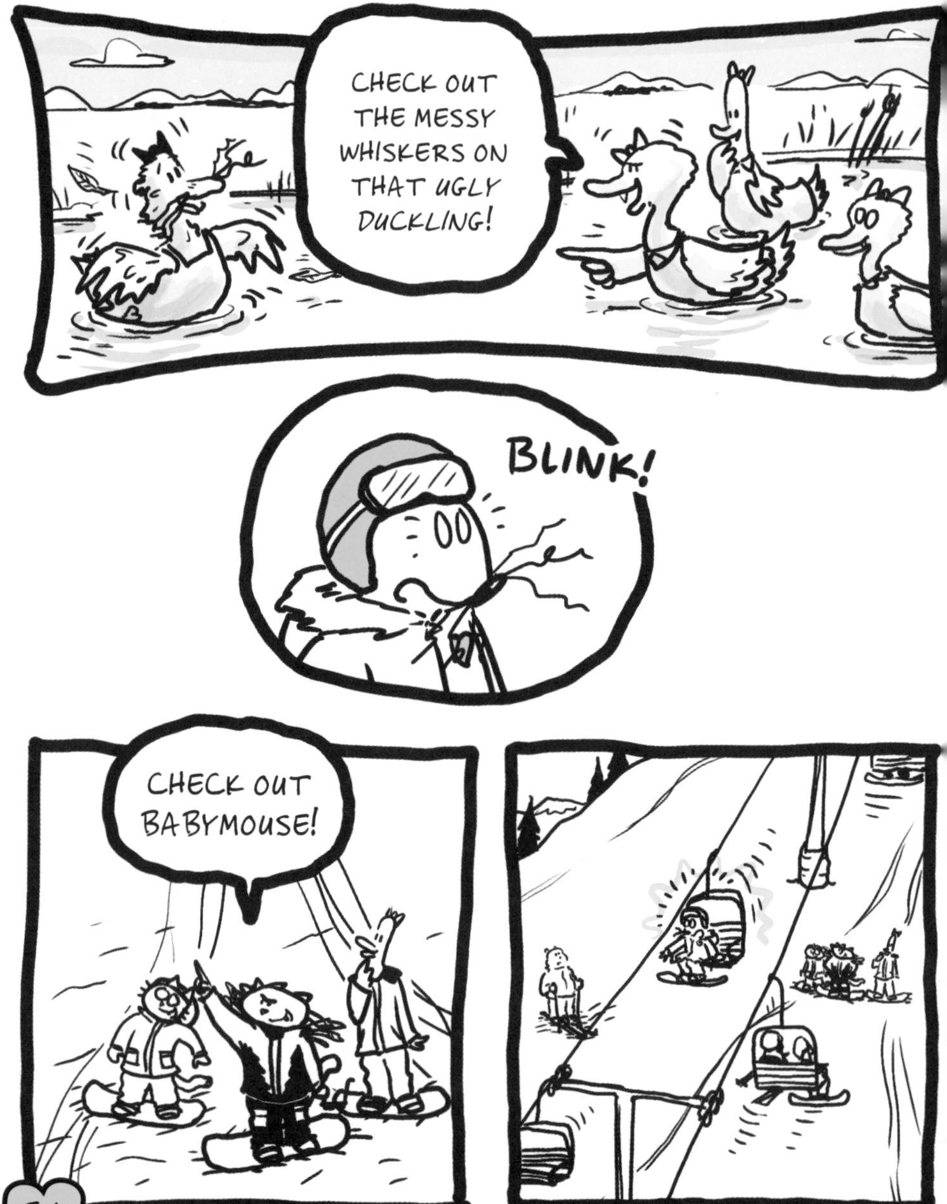
CHECK OUT THE MESSY WHISKERS ON THAT UGLY DUCKLING!
BLINK!
CHECK OUT BABYMOUSE!

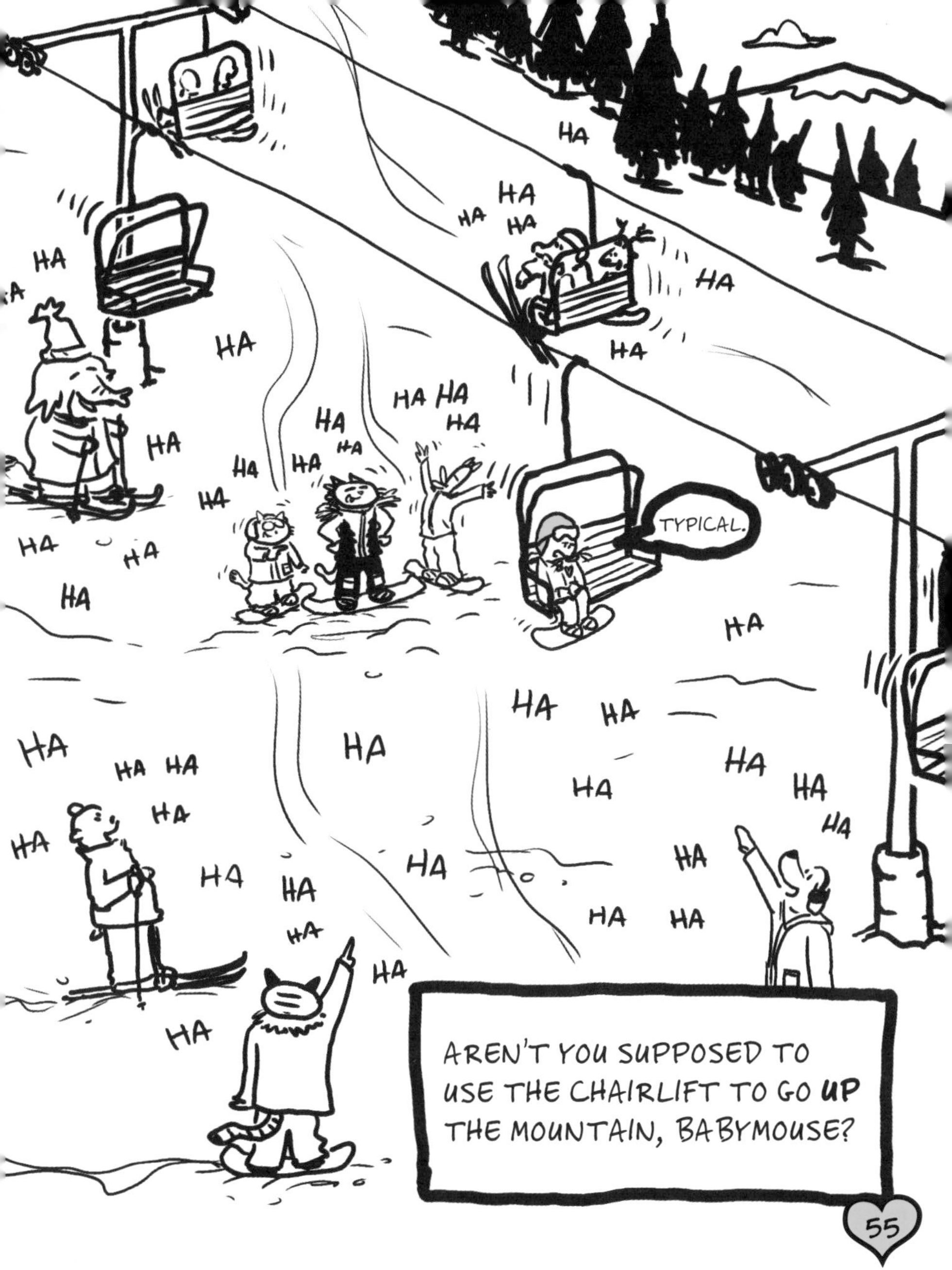
HA HA HA HA
TYPICAL.
AREN'T YOU SUPPOSED TO USE THE CHAIRLIFT TO GO **UP** THE MOUNTAIN, BABYMOUSE?

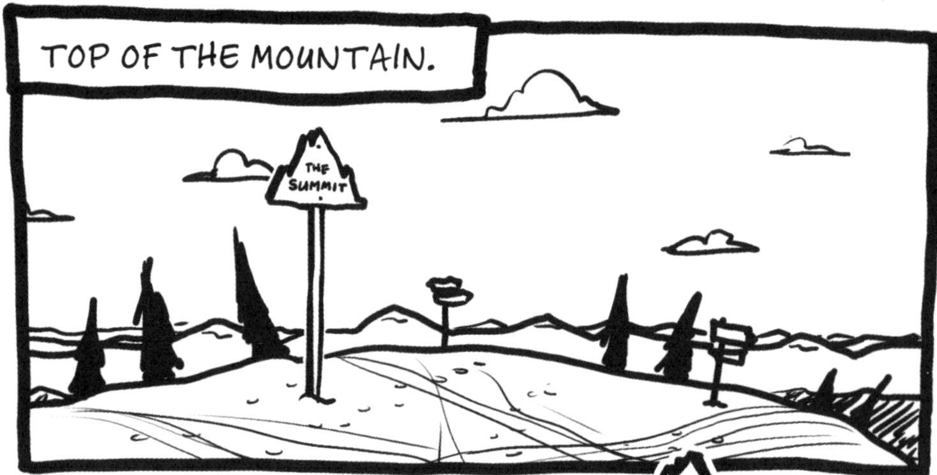
TOP OF THE MOUNTAIN.
THE SUMMIT

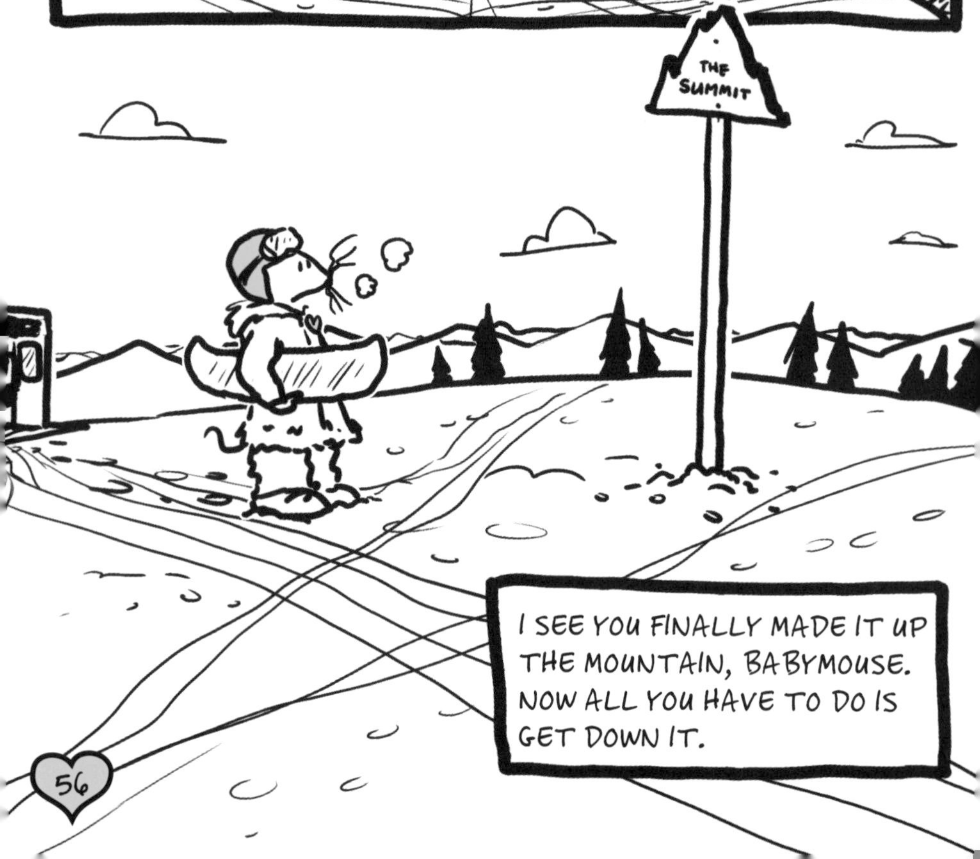
THE SUMMIT
I SEE YOU FINALLY MADE IT UP THE MOUNTAIN, BABYMOUSE. NOW ALL YOU HAVE TO DO IS GET DOWN IT.

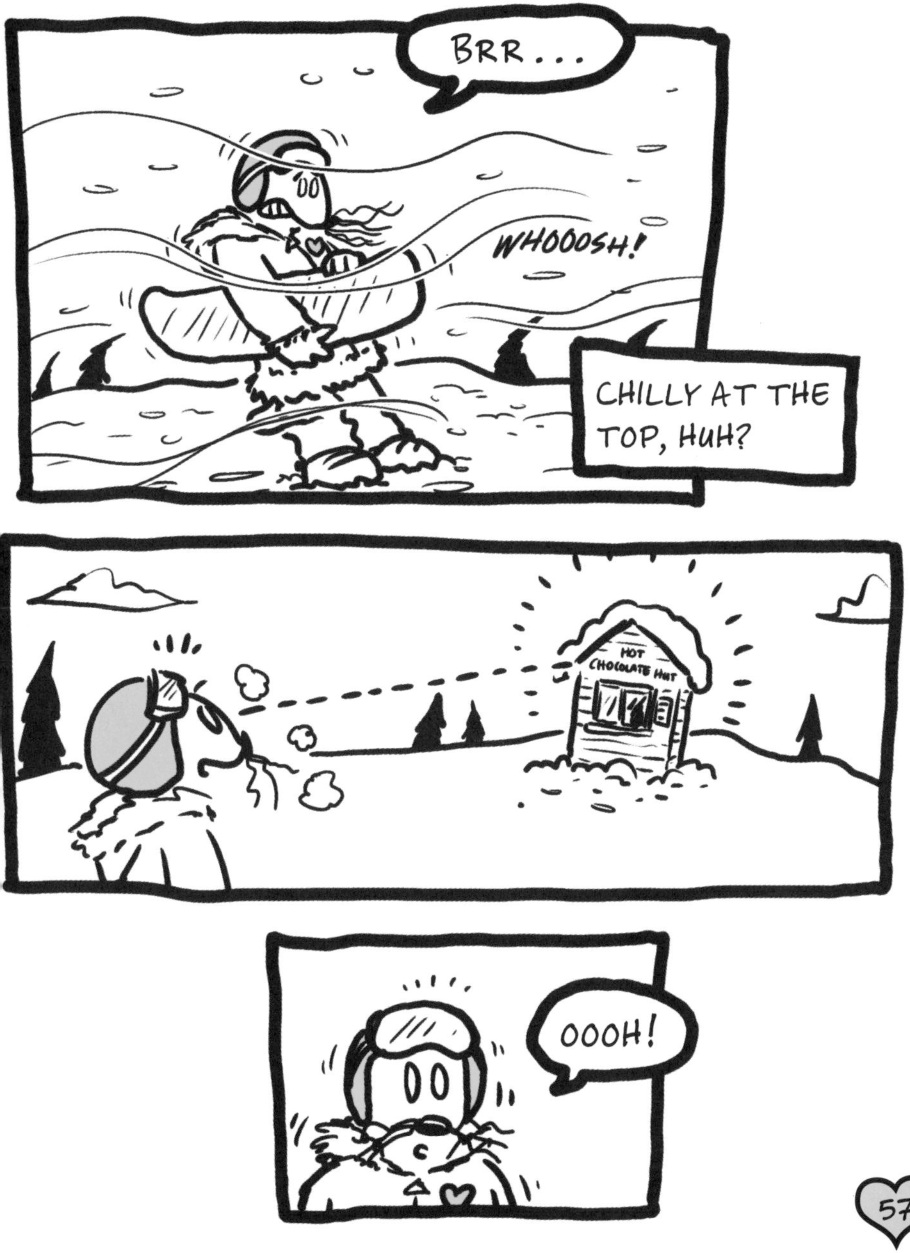
BRR...
WHOOOSH!
CHILLY AT THE TOP, HUH?
HOT CHOCOLATE HUT
OOOH!

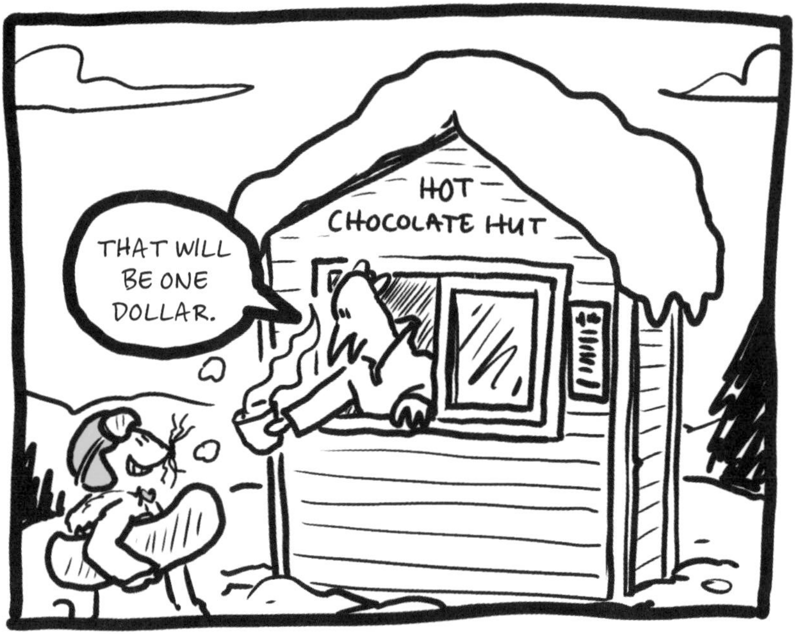
HOT CHOCOLATE HUT
THAT WILL BE ONE DOLLAR.

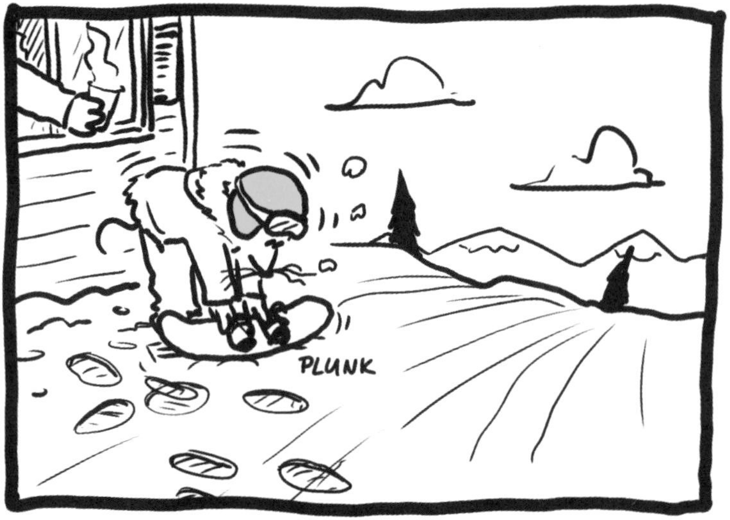
PLUNK

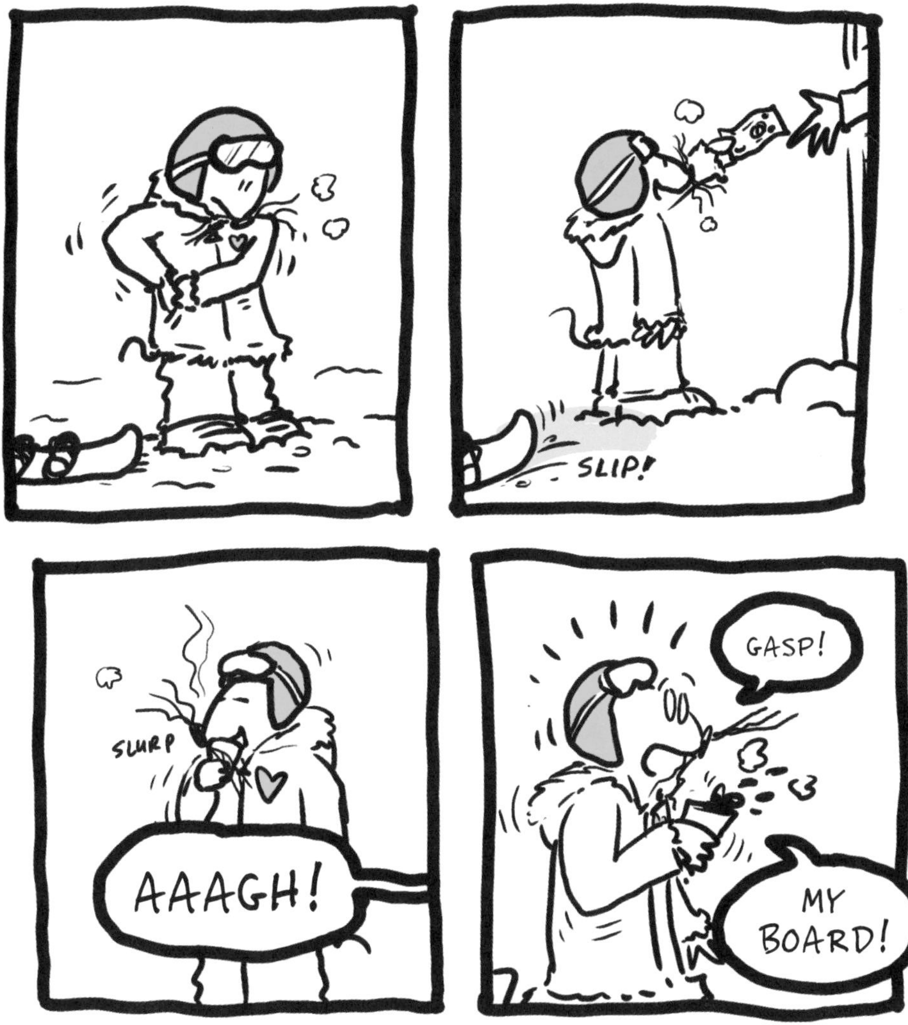
SLIP!
SLURP
AAAGH!
GASP!
MY BOARD!

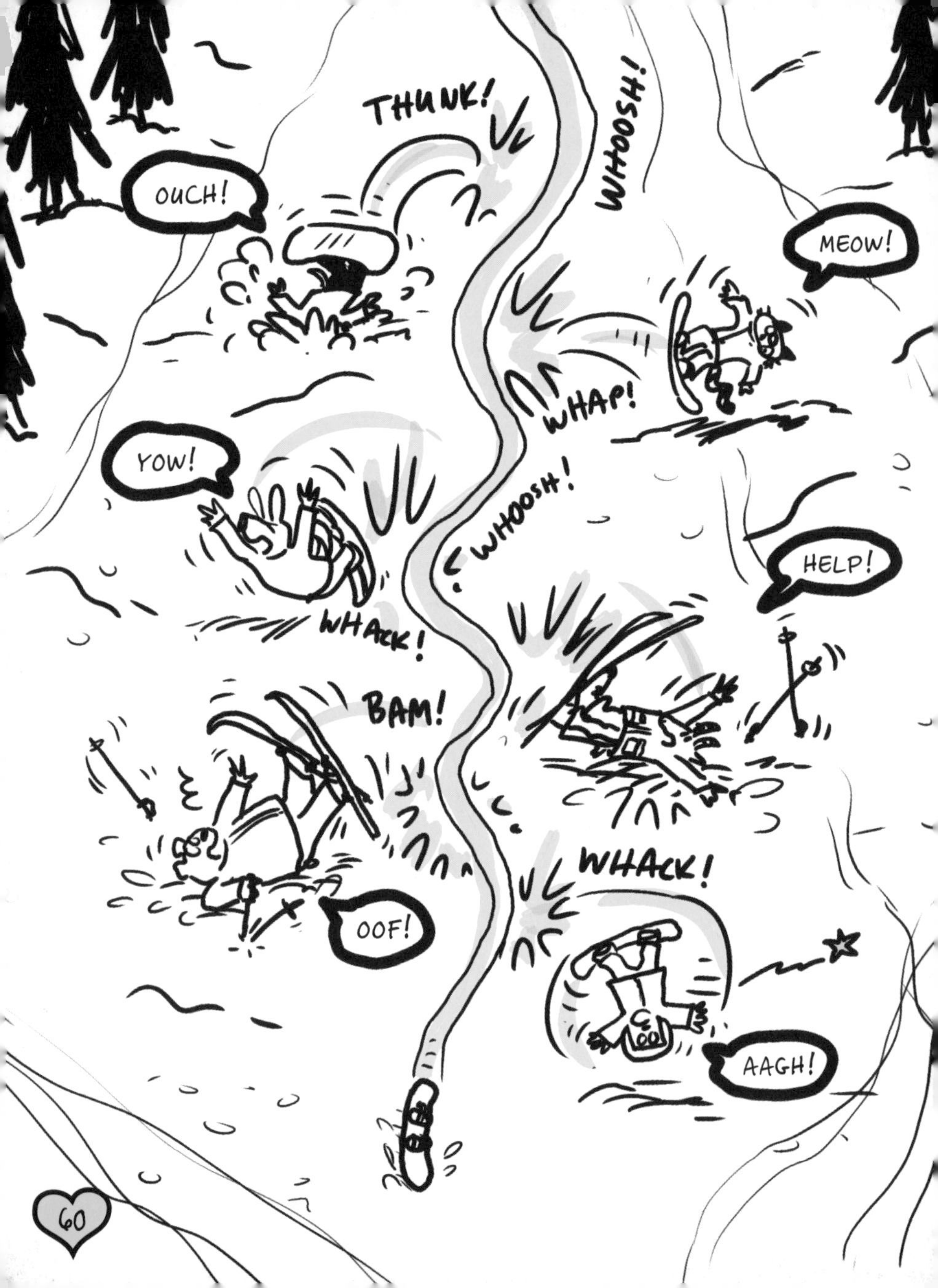
THUNK!
OUCH!
WHOOSH!
MEOW!
WHAP!
YOW!
WHOOSH!
HELP!
WHACK!
BAM!
WHACK!
OOF!
AAGH!

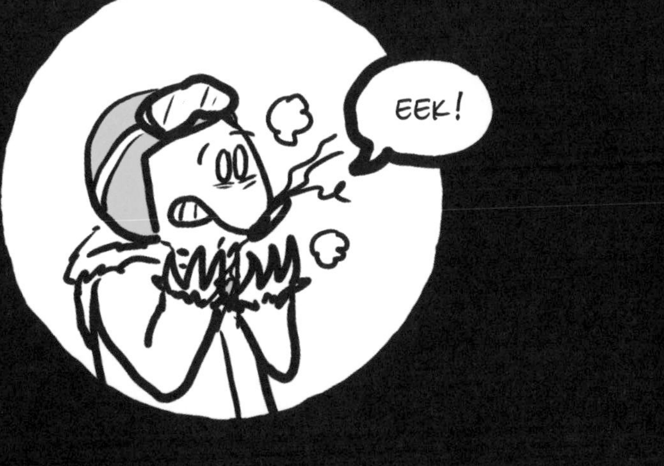
EEK!
AT LEAST YOUR **BOARD** MADE IT DOWN THE MOUNTAIN, BABYMOUSE.

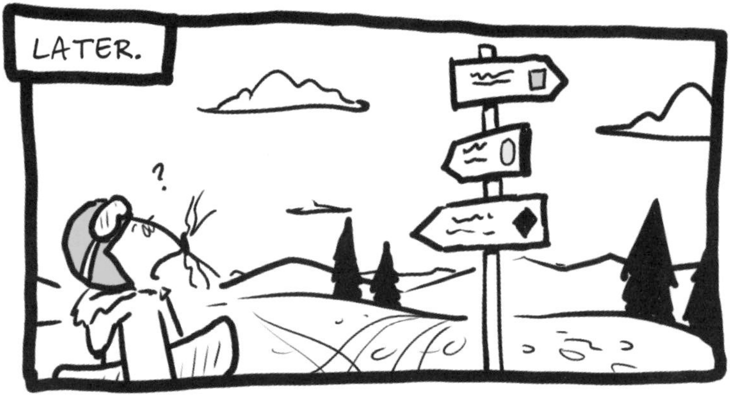
LATER.
?

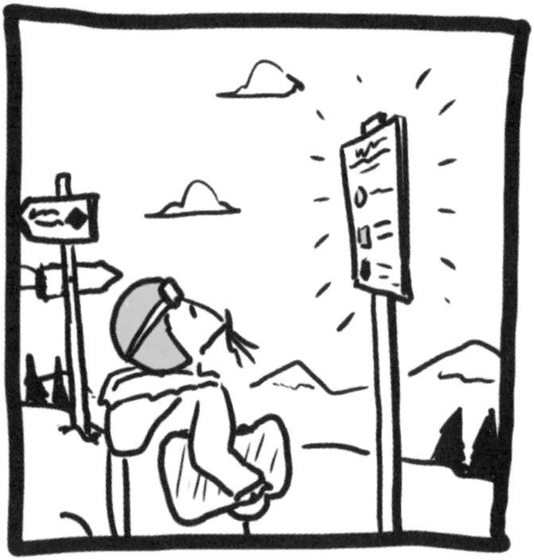

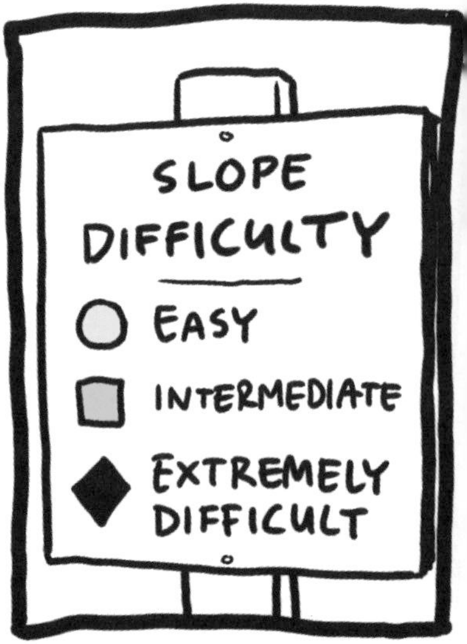
SLOPE DIFFICULTY
EASY
INTERMEDIATE
EXTREMELY DIFFICULT

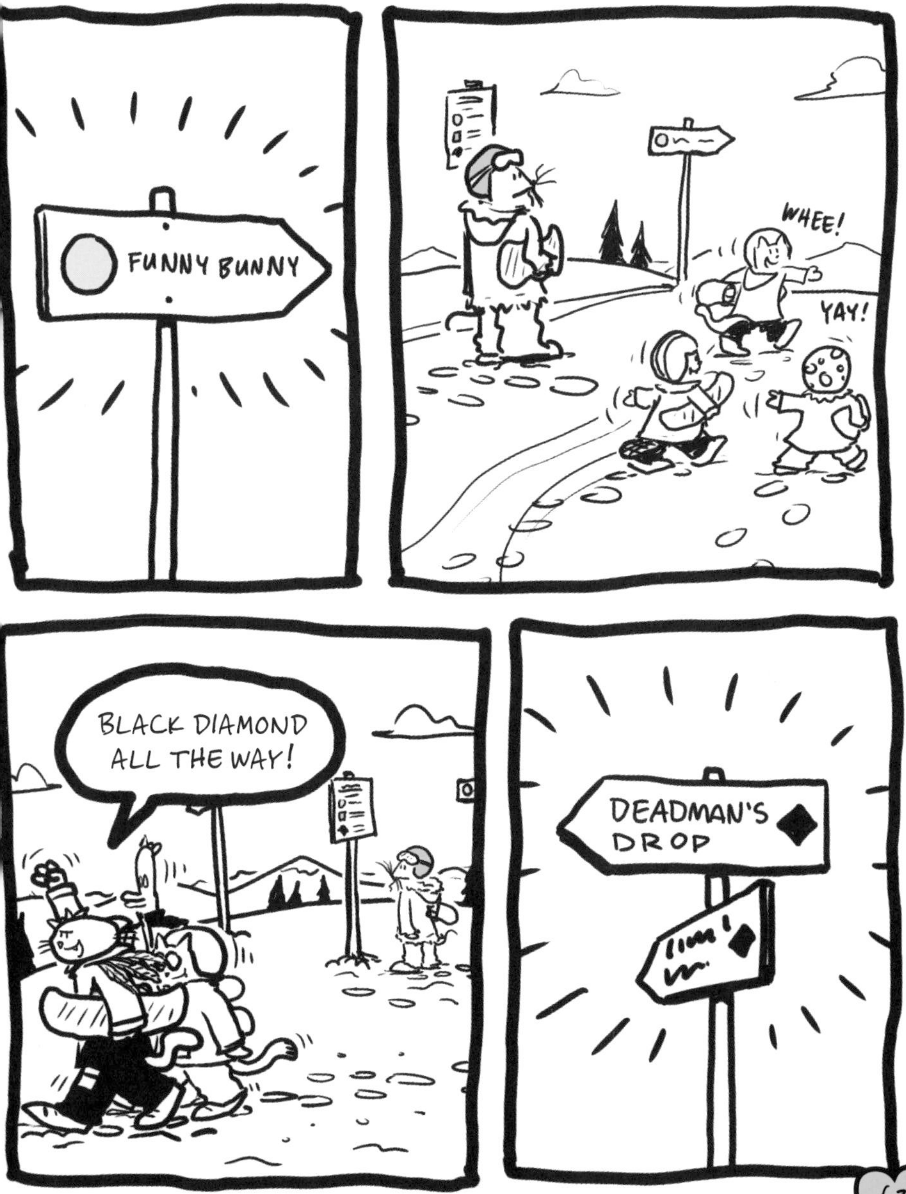
FUNNY BUNNY
WHEE!
YAY!
BLACK DIAMOND ALL THE WAY!
DEADMAN'S DROP

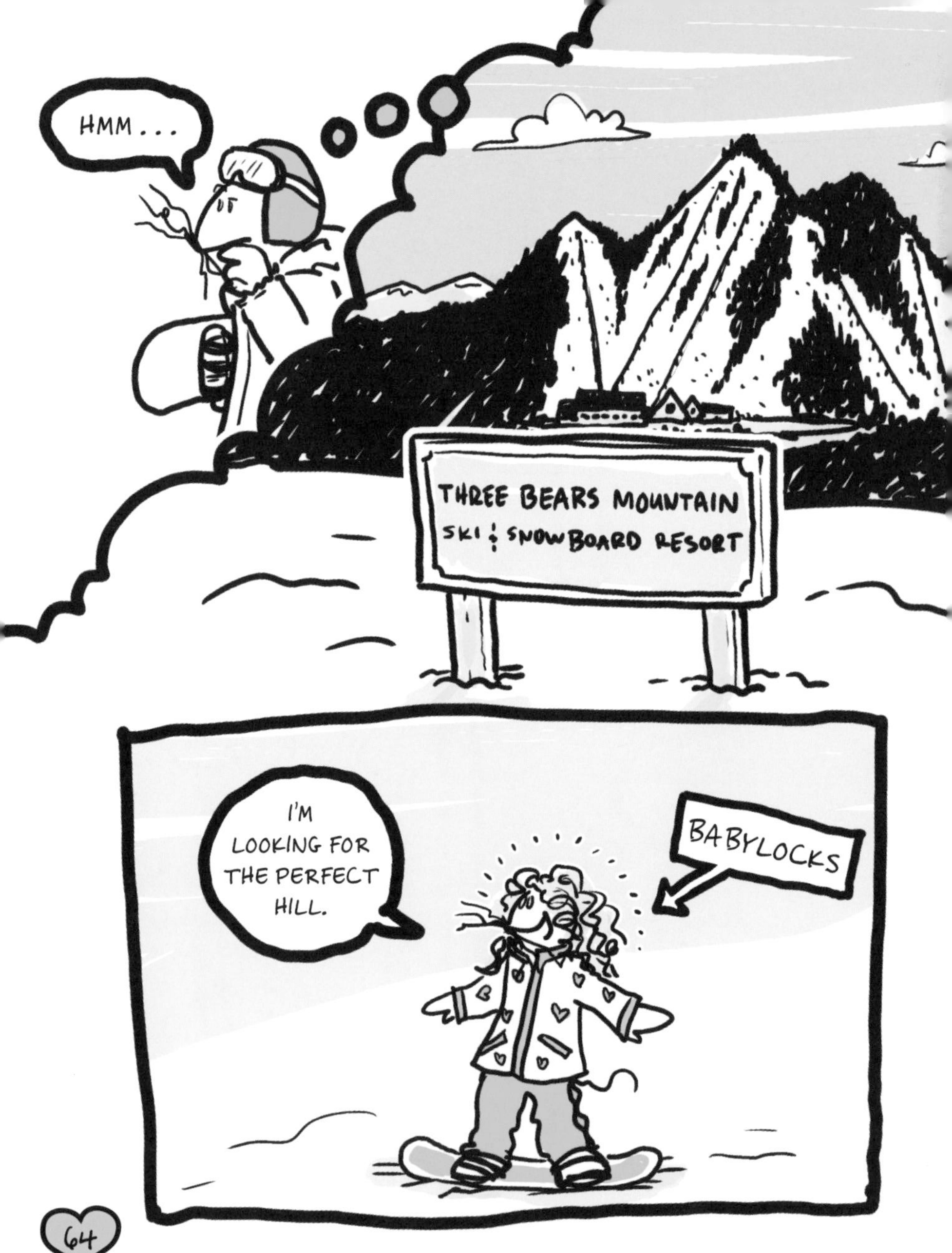
HMM...
THREE BEARS MOUNTAIN
SKI & SNOWBOARD RESORT
I'M LOOKING FOR THE PERFECT HILL.
BABYLOCKS

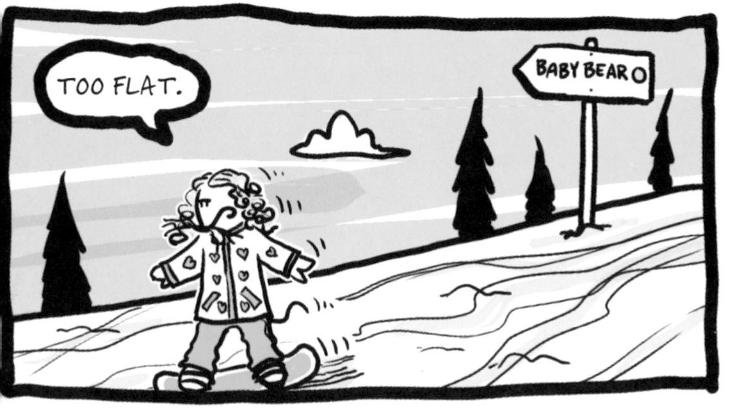
TOO FLAT.
BABY BEAR

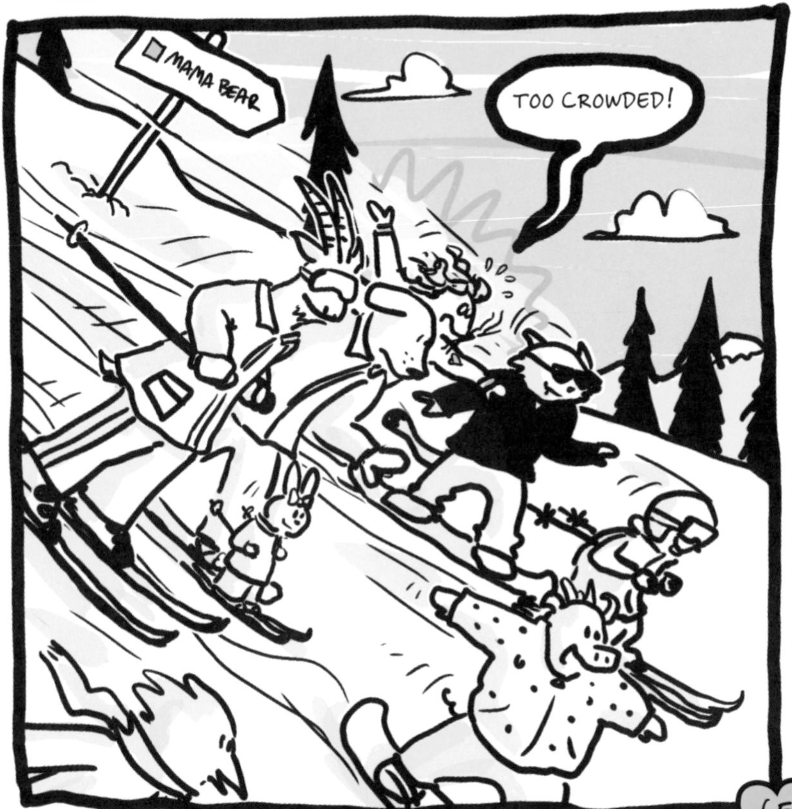
MAMA BEAR
TOO CROWDED!

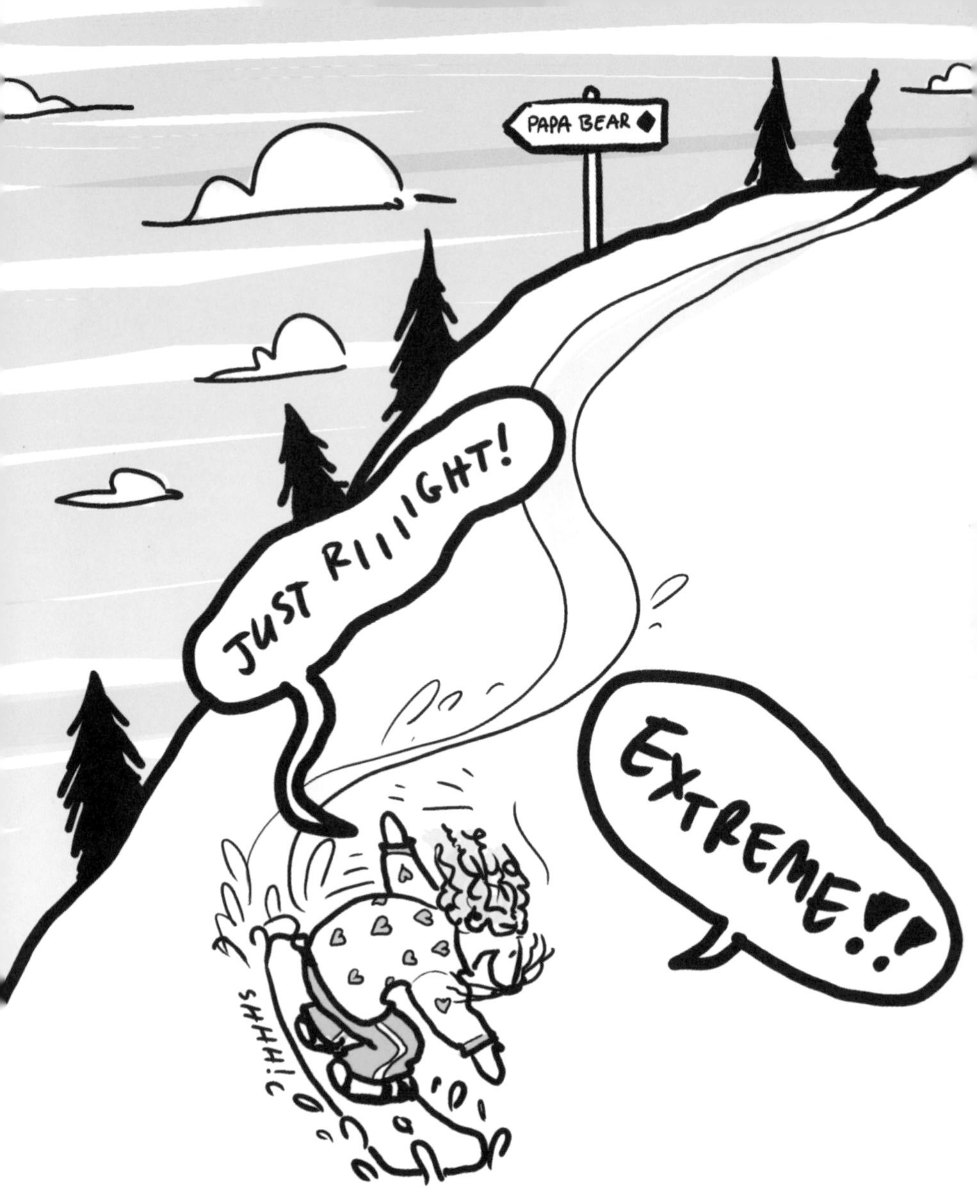
PAPA BEAR
JUST RIIIIGHT!
EXTREME!!
SHHH!

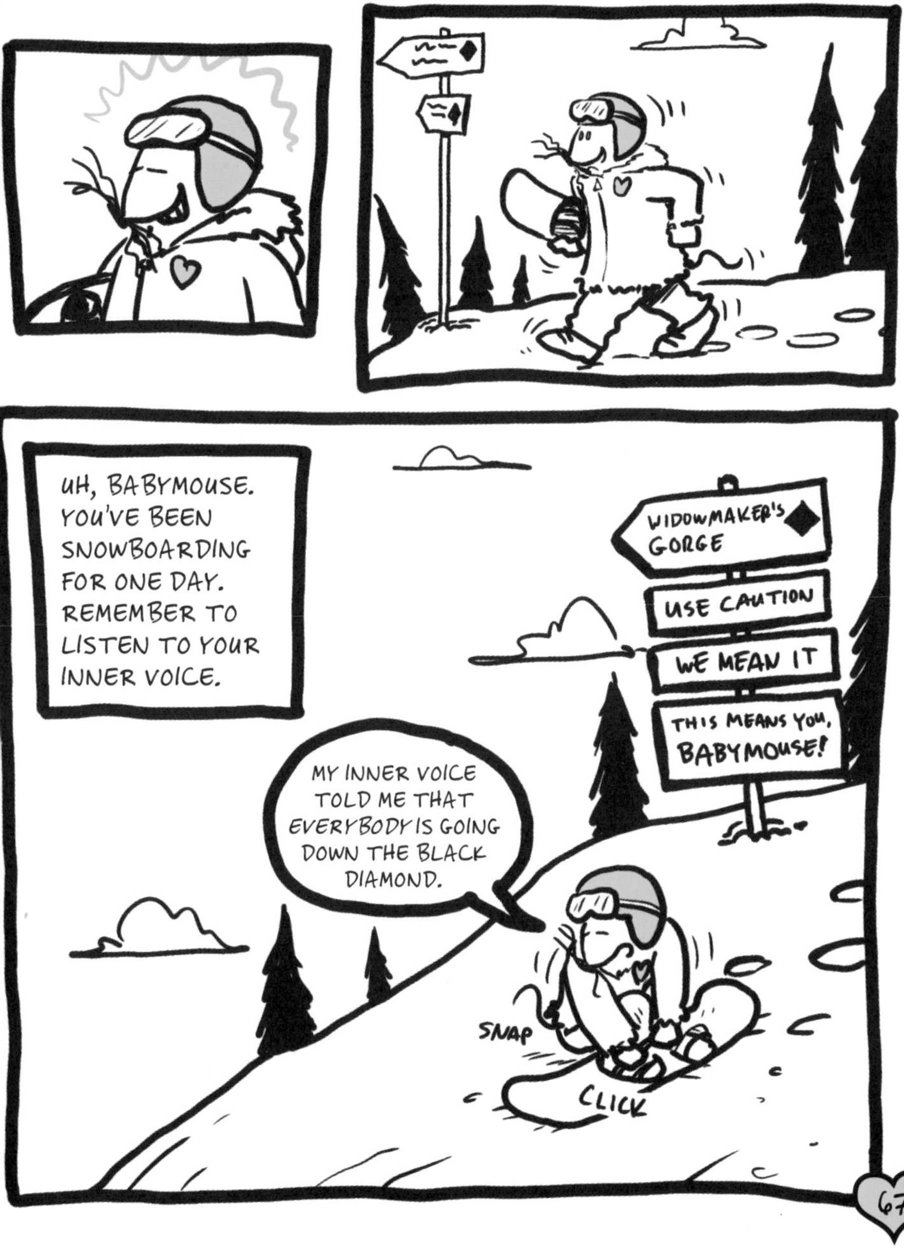
UH, BABYMOUSE. YOU'VE BEEN SNOWBOARDING FOR ONE DAY. REMEMBER TO LISTEN TO YOUR INNER VOICE.
WIDOWMAKER'S GORGE
USE CAUTION
WE MEAN IT
THIS MEANS YOU, BABYMOUSE!
MY INNER VOICE TOLD ME THAT EVERYBODY IS GOING DOWN THE BLACK DIAMOND.
SNAP
CLICK

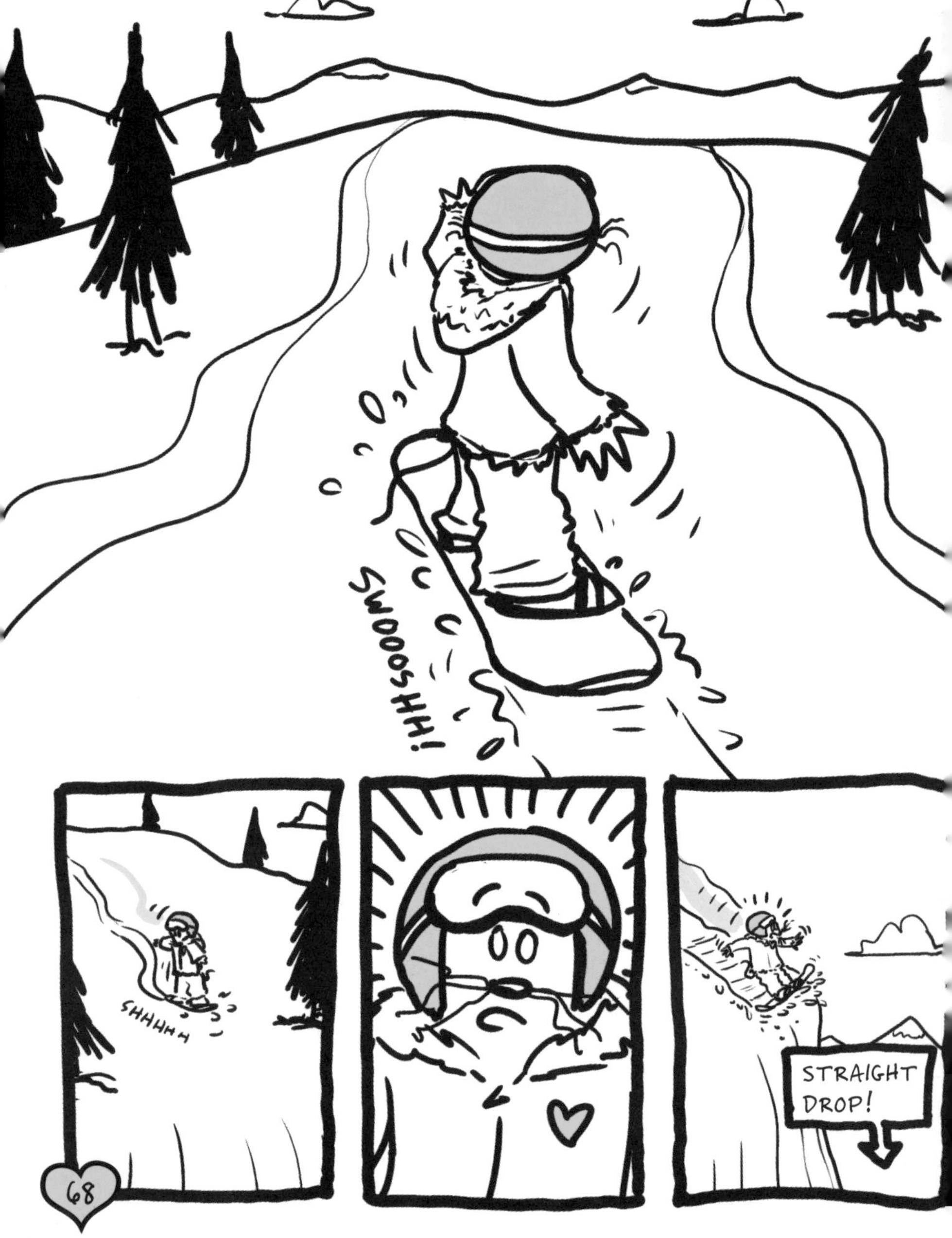
SWOOOSHH!
SHHHHH
STRAIGHT DROP!

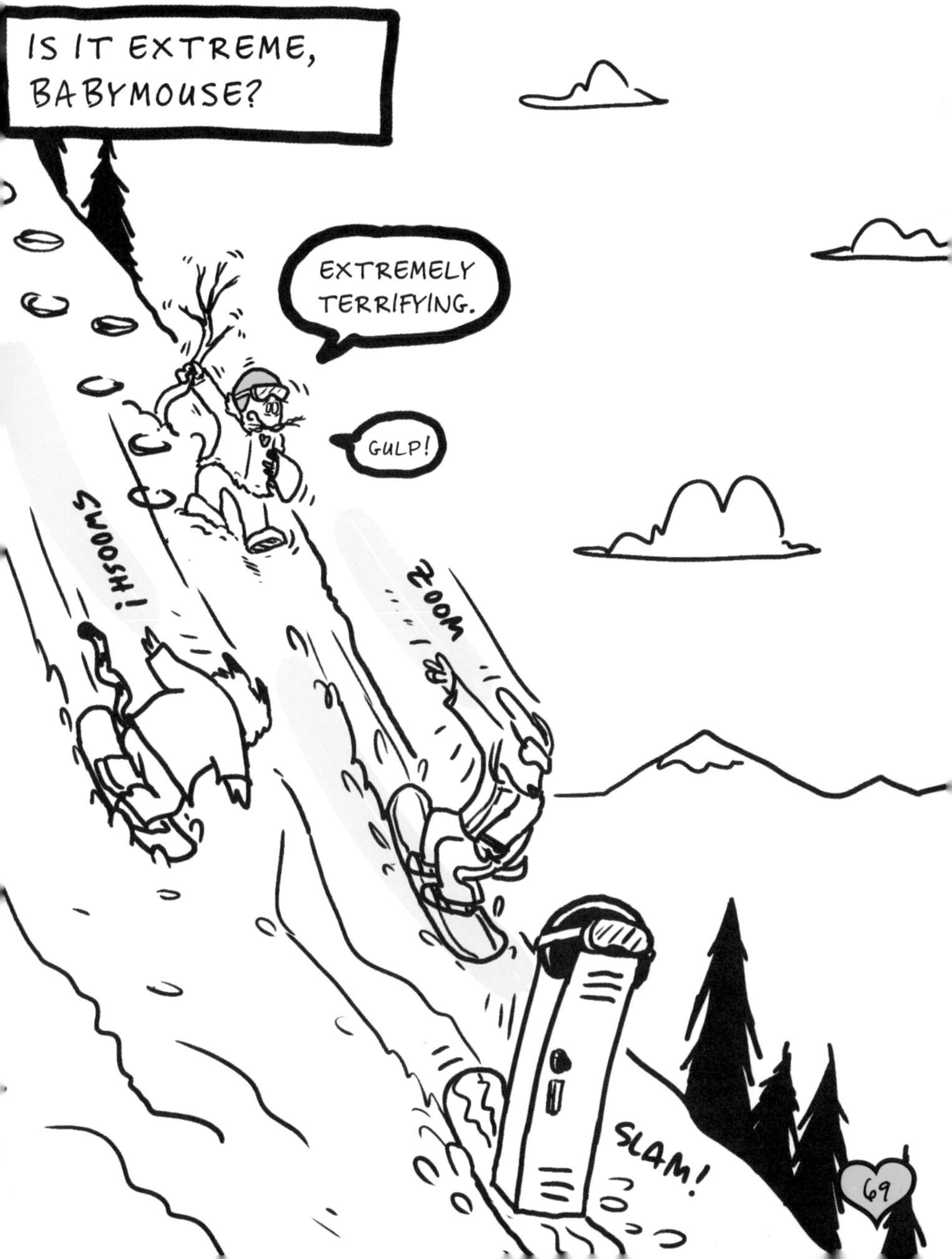
IS IT EXTREME, BABYMOUSE?
EXTREMELY TERRIFYING.
GULP!
SWOOSH!
ZOOM
SLAM!

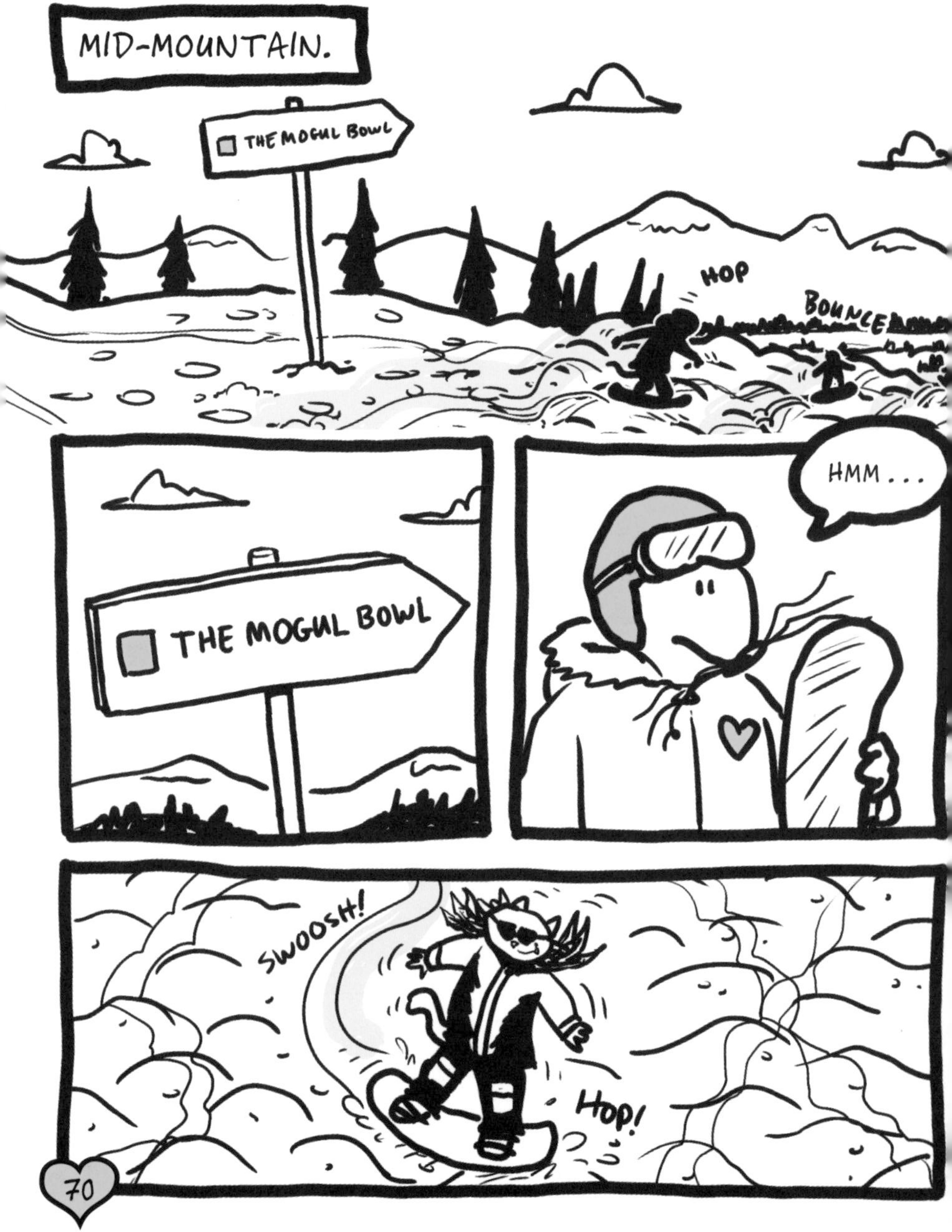
MID-MOUNTAIN.
THE MOGUL BOWL
HOP
BOUNCE
THE MOGUL BOWL
HMM...
SWOOSH!
HOP!

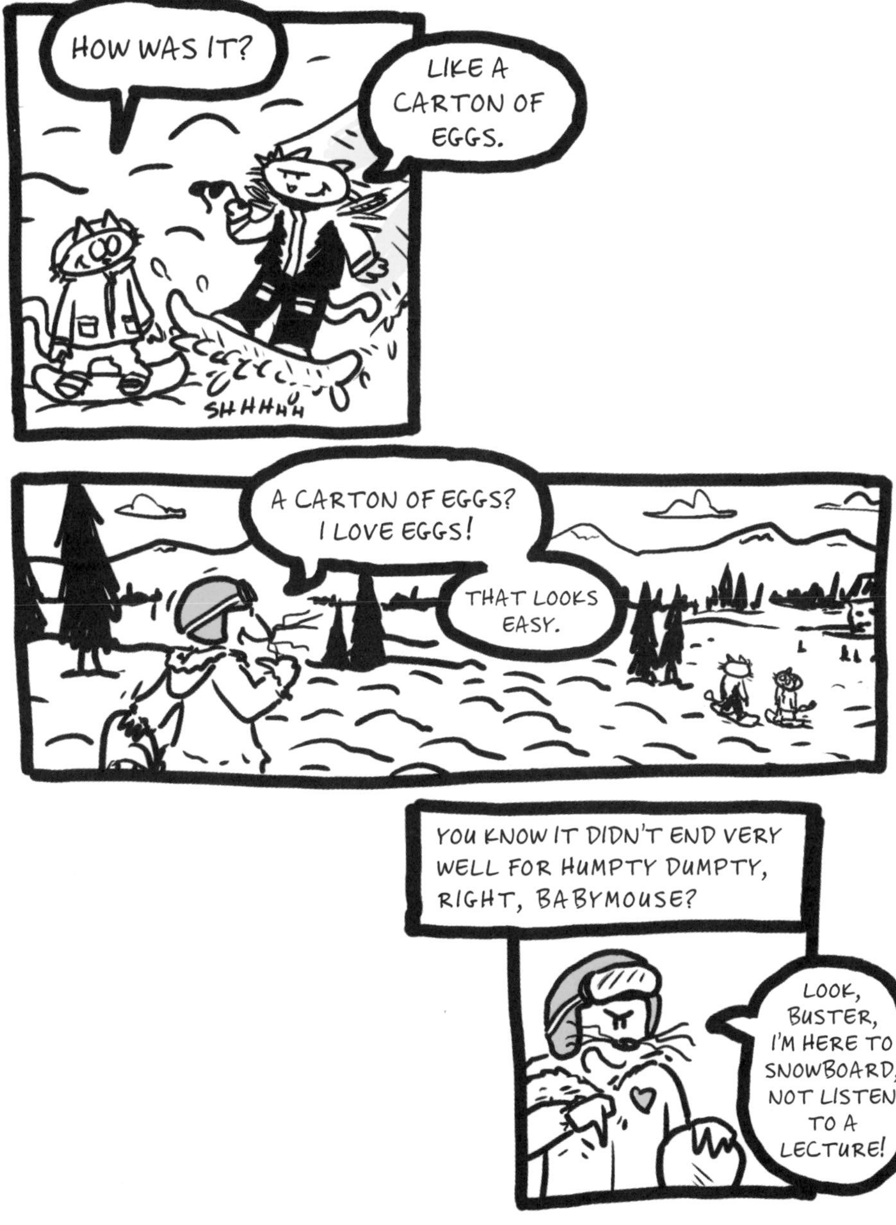
HOW WAS IT?
LIKE A CARTON OF EGGS.
SHHHHH
A CARTON OF EGGS? I LOVE EGGS!
THAT LOOKS EASY.
YOU KNOW IT DIDN'T END VERY WELL FOR HUMPTY DUMPTY, RIGHT, BABYMOUSE?
LOOK, BUSTER, I'M HERE TO SNOWBOARD, NOT LISTEN TO A LECTURE!

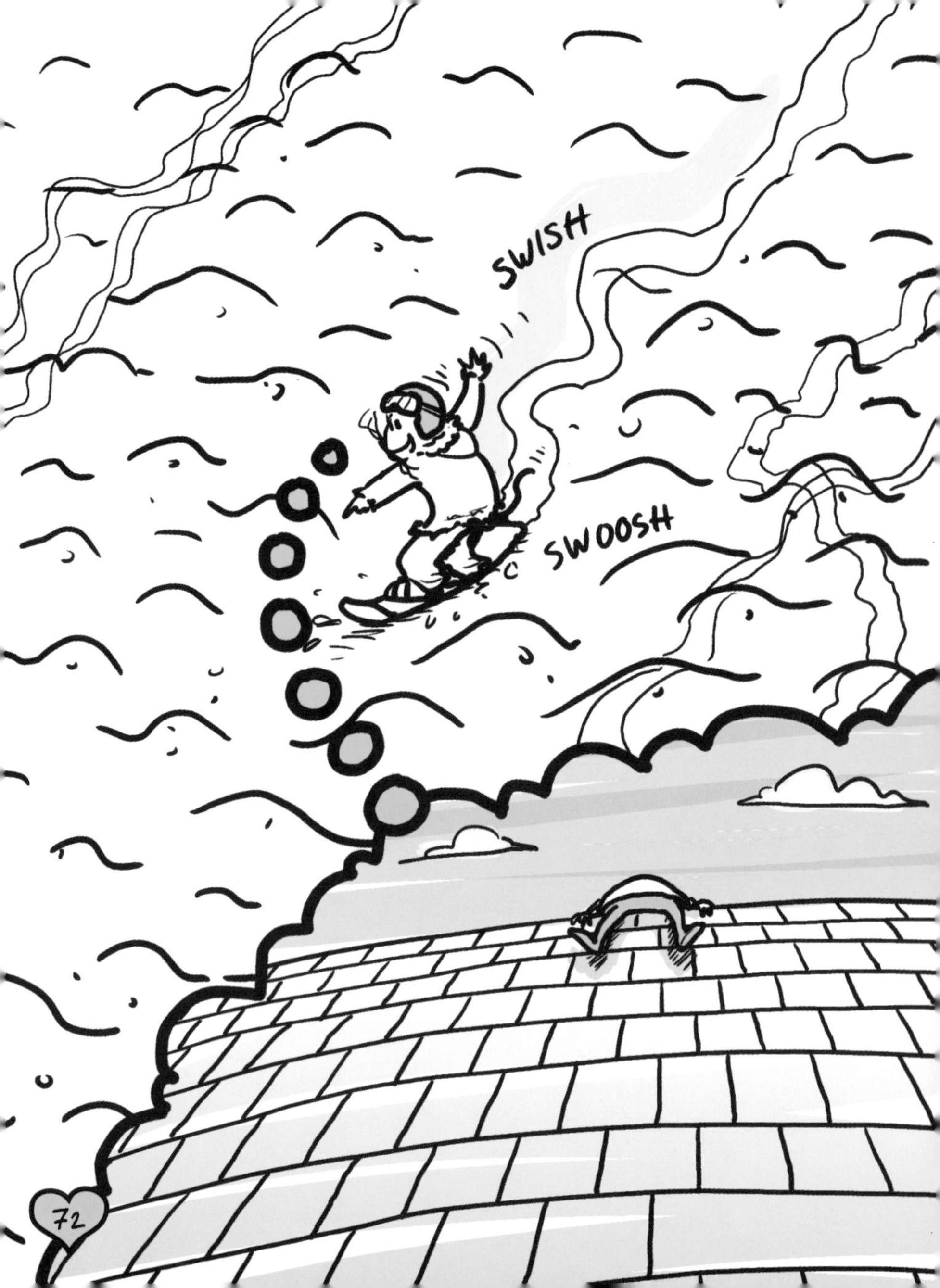
SWISH
SWOOSH

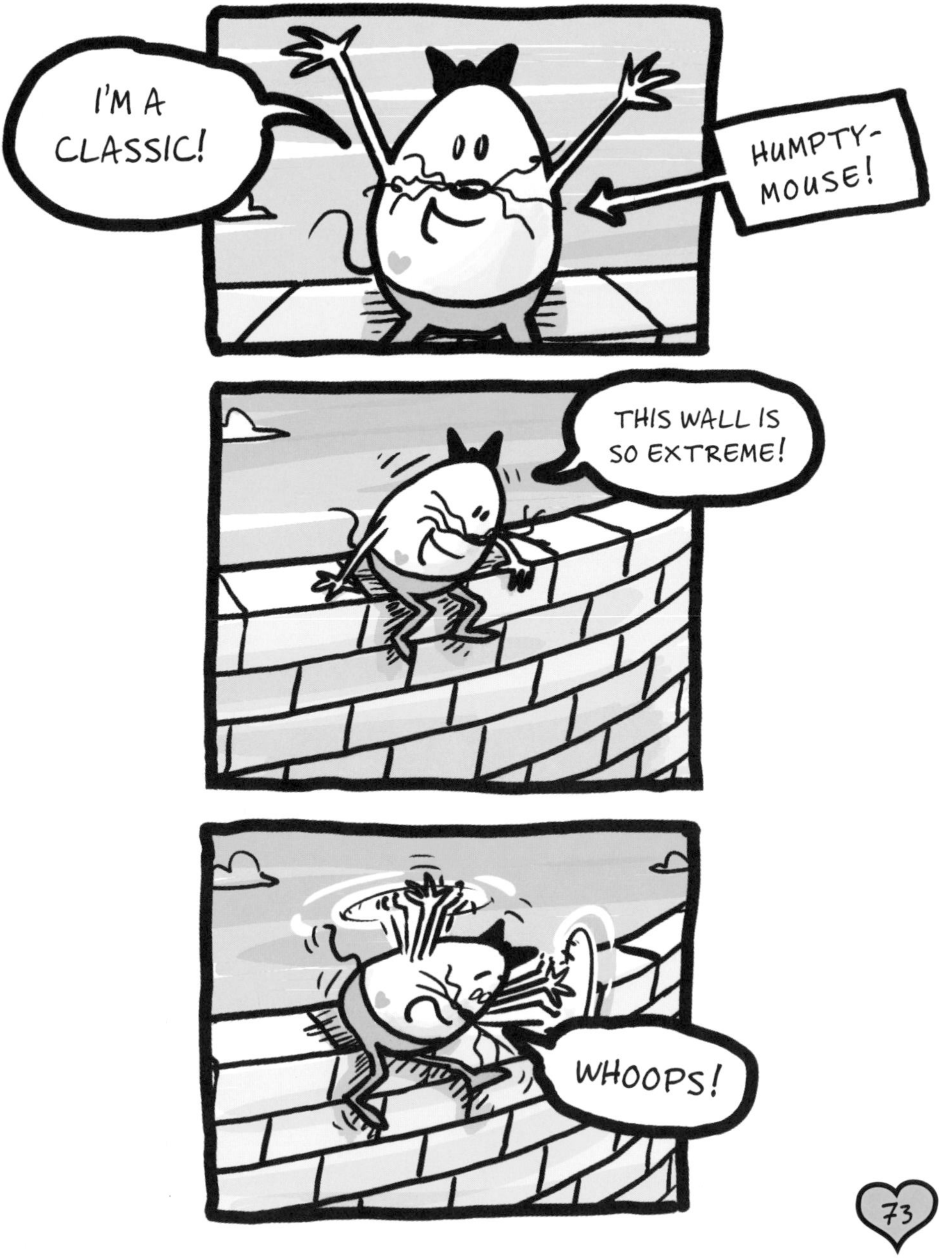
I'M A CLASSIC!
HUMPTY-MOUSE!
THIS WALL IS SO EXTREME!
WHOOPS!

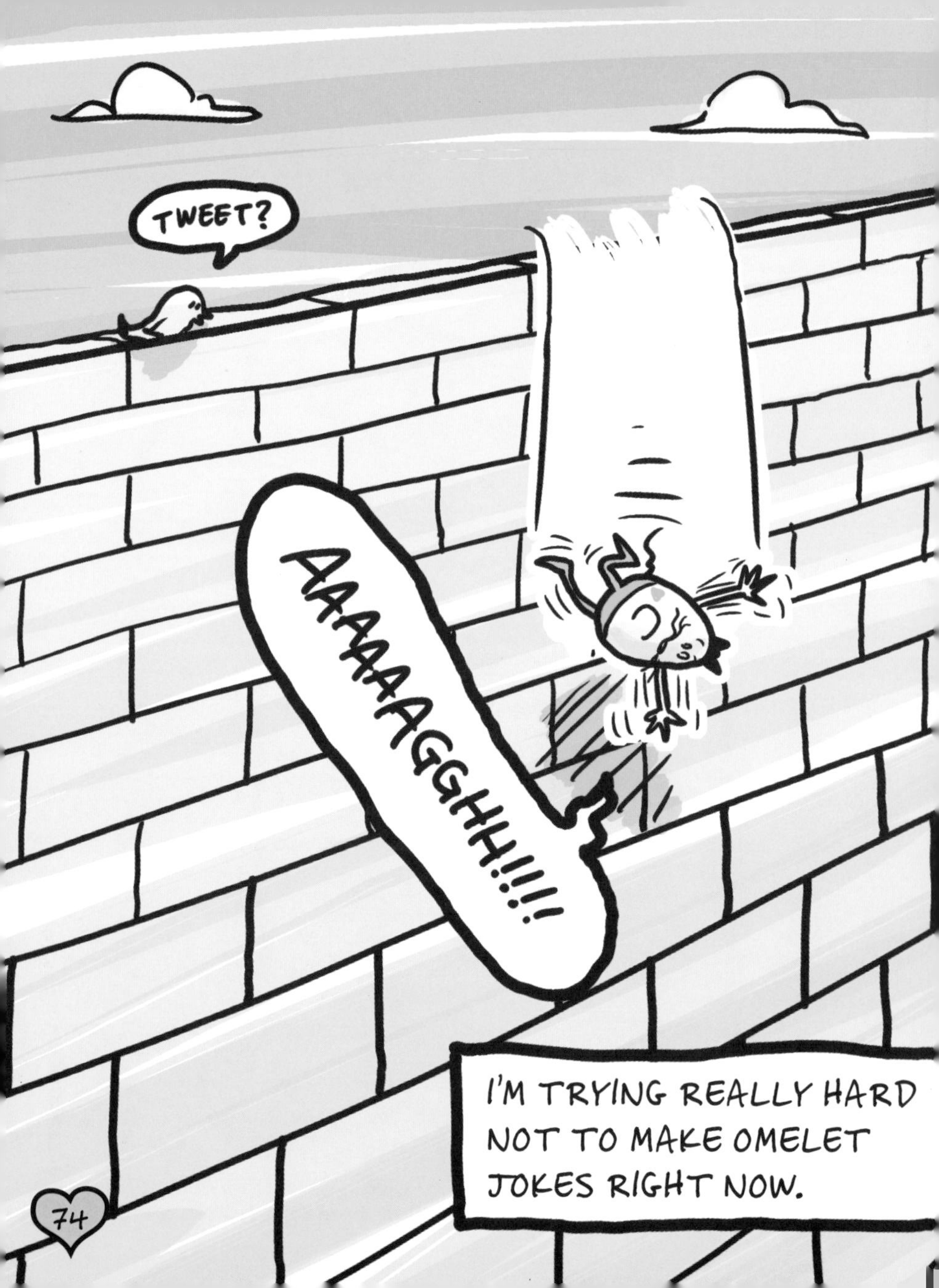
TWEET?
AAAAAAGGHH!!!!!
I'M TRYING REALLY HARD NOT TO MAKE OMELET JOKES RIGHT NOW.

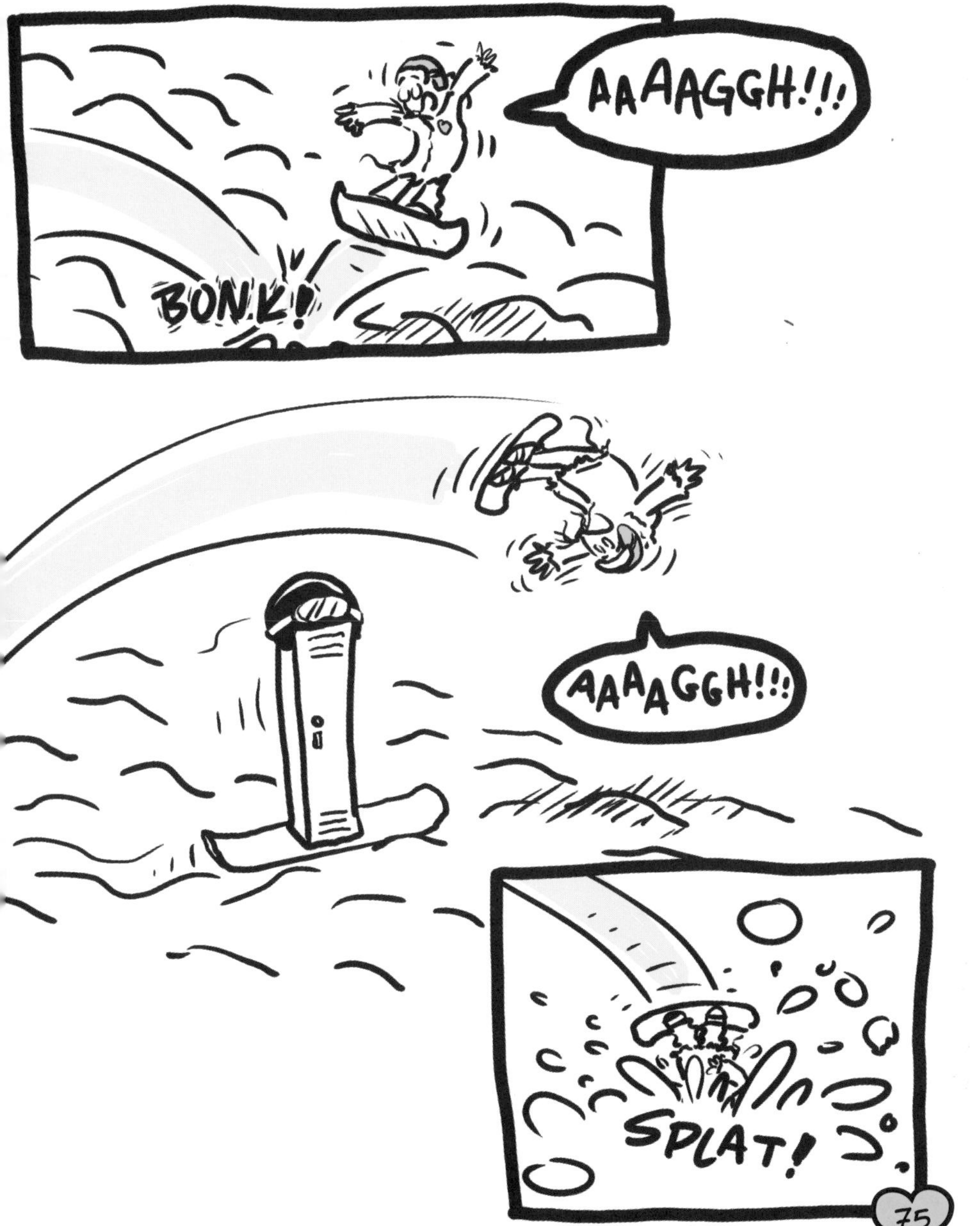
AAAAGGH!!!
BONK!
AAAAGGH!!!
SPLAT!

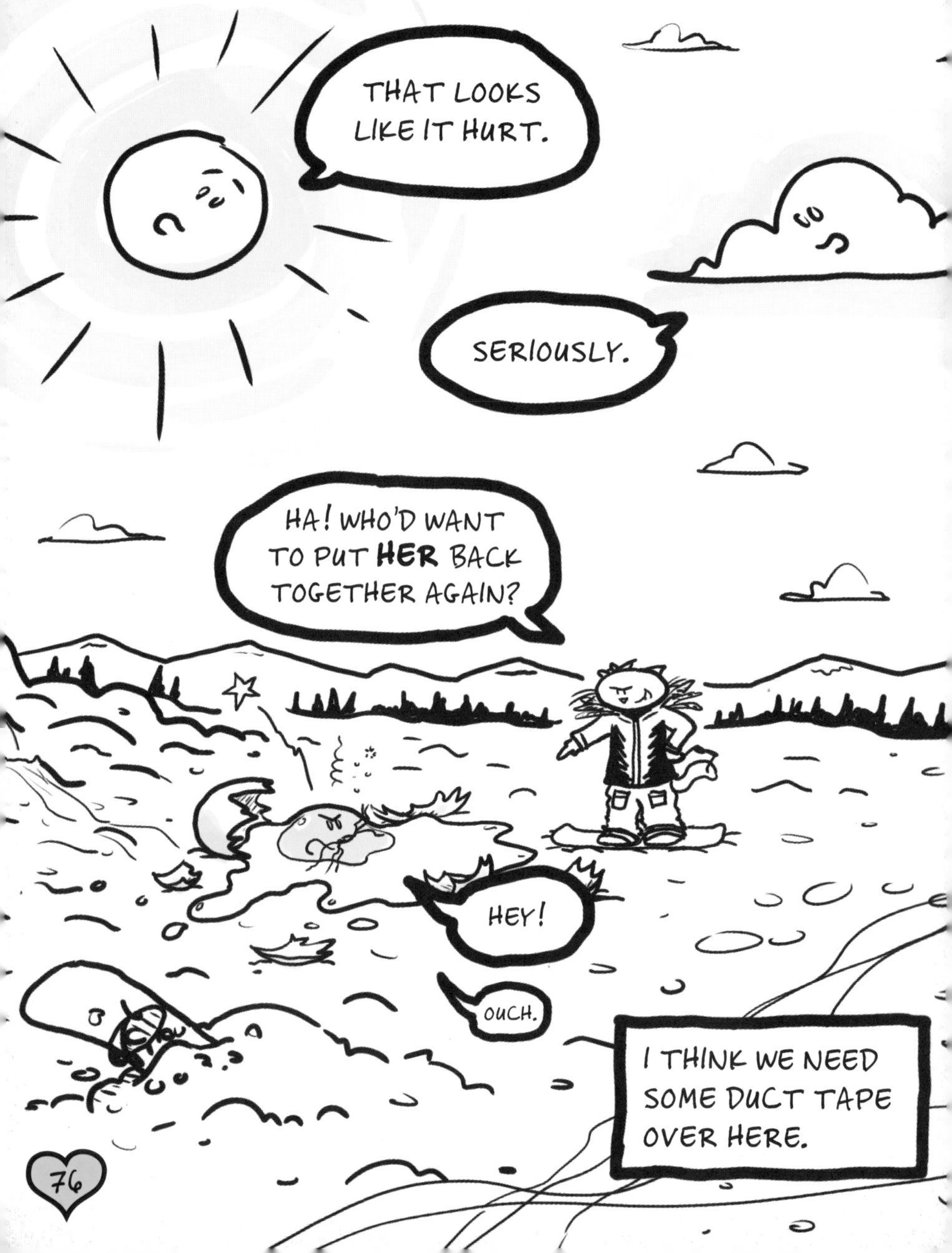
THAT LOOKS LIKE IT HURT.
SERIOUSLY.
HA! WHO'D WANT TO PUT **HER** BACK TOGETHER AGAIN?
HEY!
OUCH.
I THINK WE NEED SOME DUCT TAPE OVER HERE.

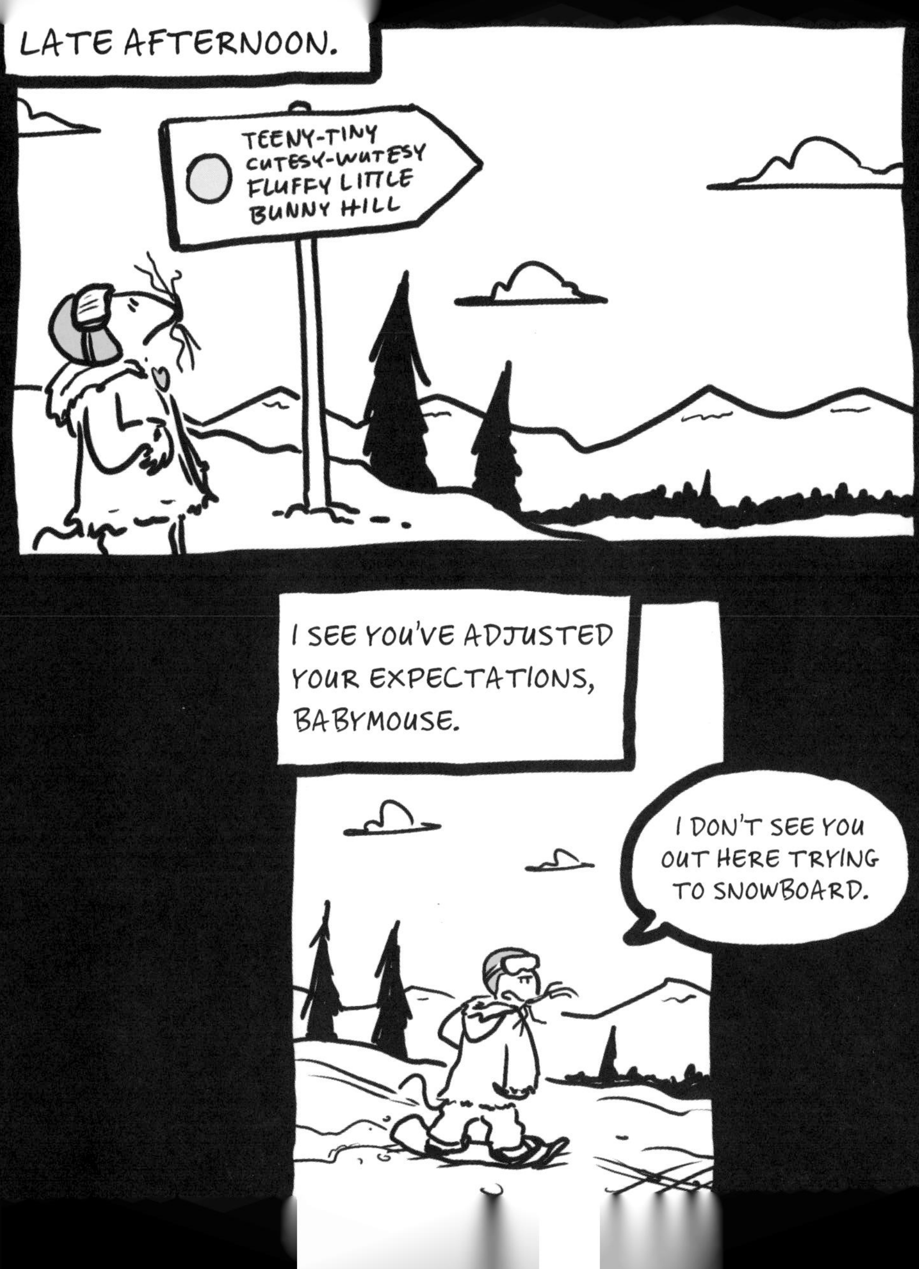
LATE AFTERNOON.
TEENY-TINY CUTESY-WUTESY FLUFFY LITTLE BUNNY HILL
I SEE YOU'VE ADJUSTED YOUR EXPECTATIONS, BABYMOUSE.
I DON'T SEE YOU OUT HERE TRYING TO SNOWBOARD.

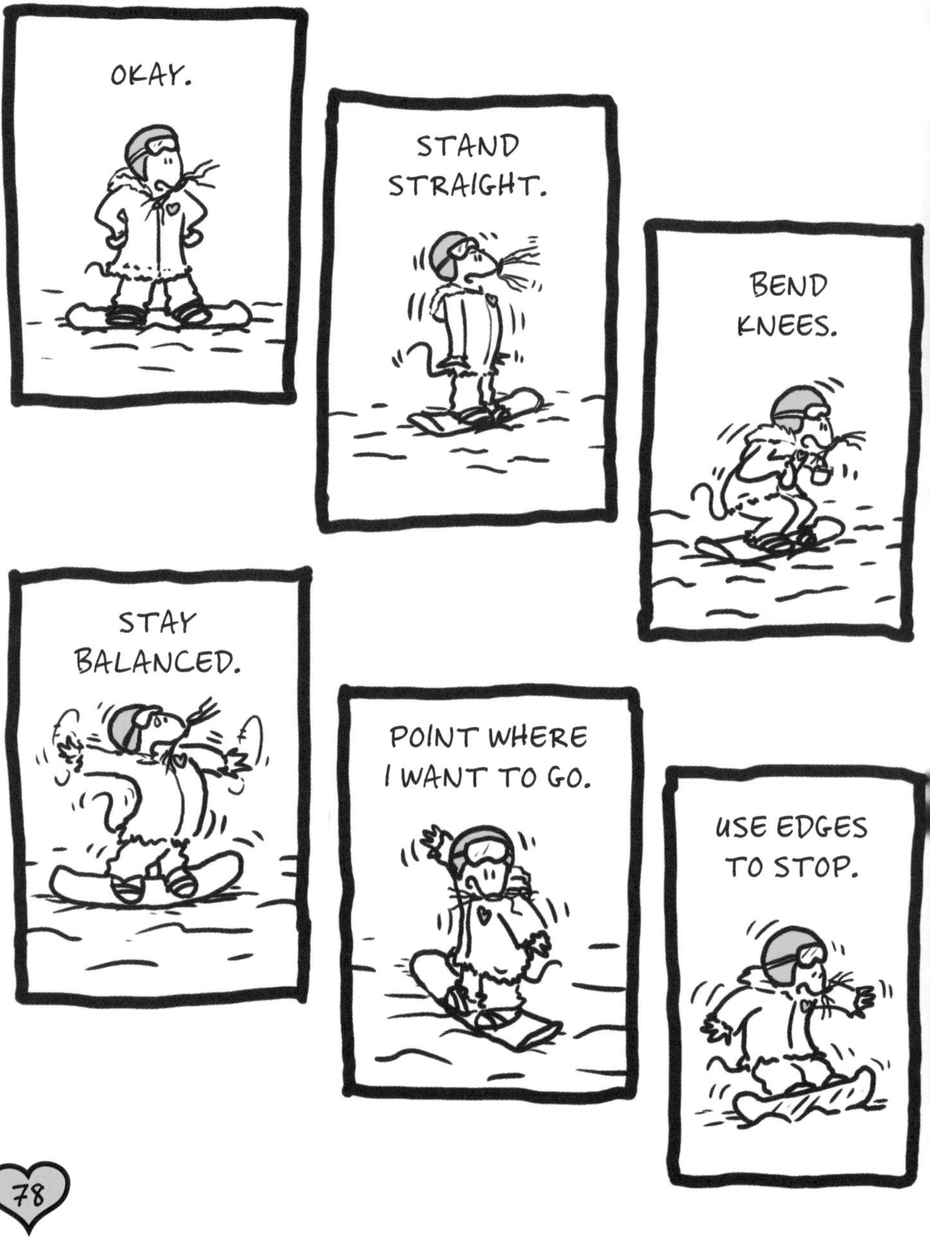
OKAY.
STAND STRAIGHT.
BEND KNEES.
STAY BALANCED.
POINT WHERE I WANT TO GO.
USE EDGES TO STOP.

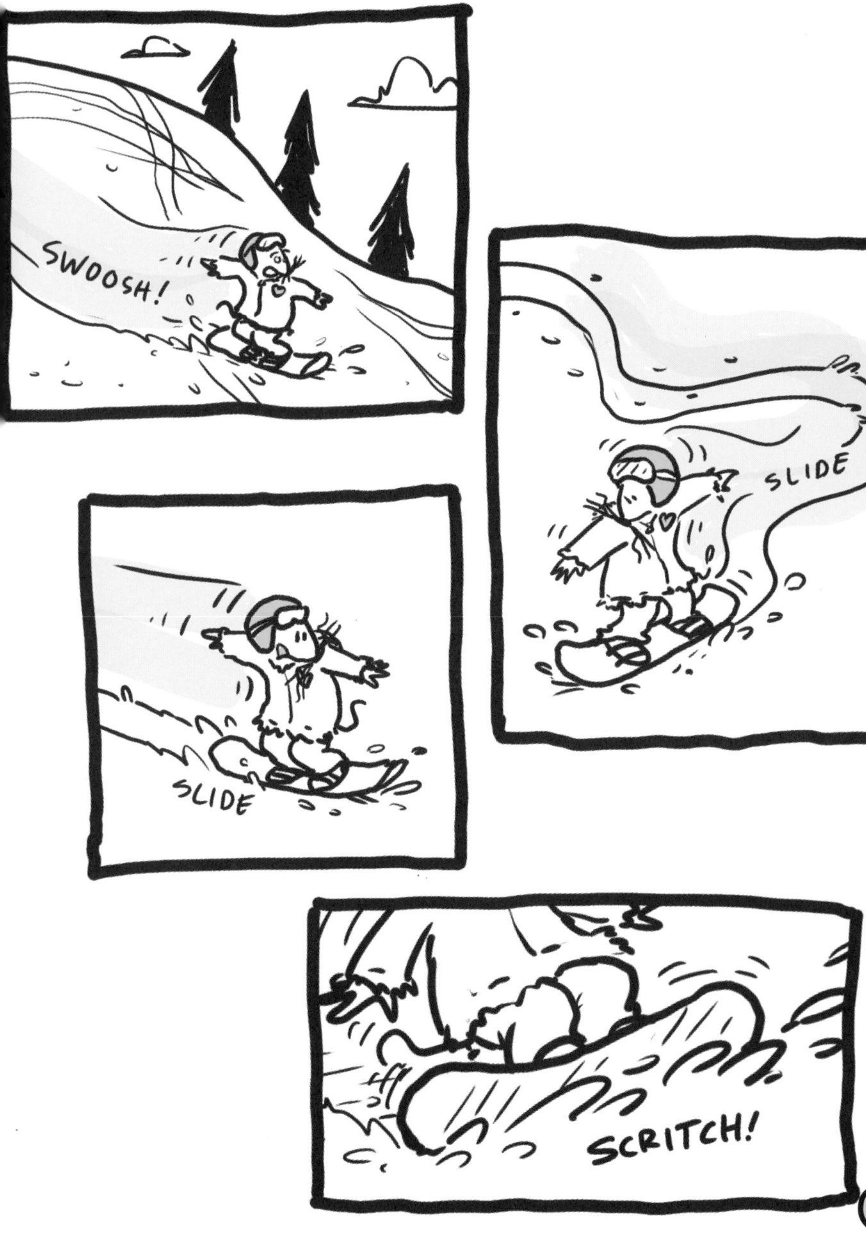
SWOOSH!
SLIDE
SLIDE
SCRITCH!

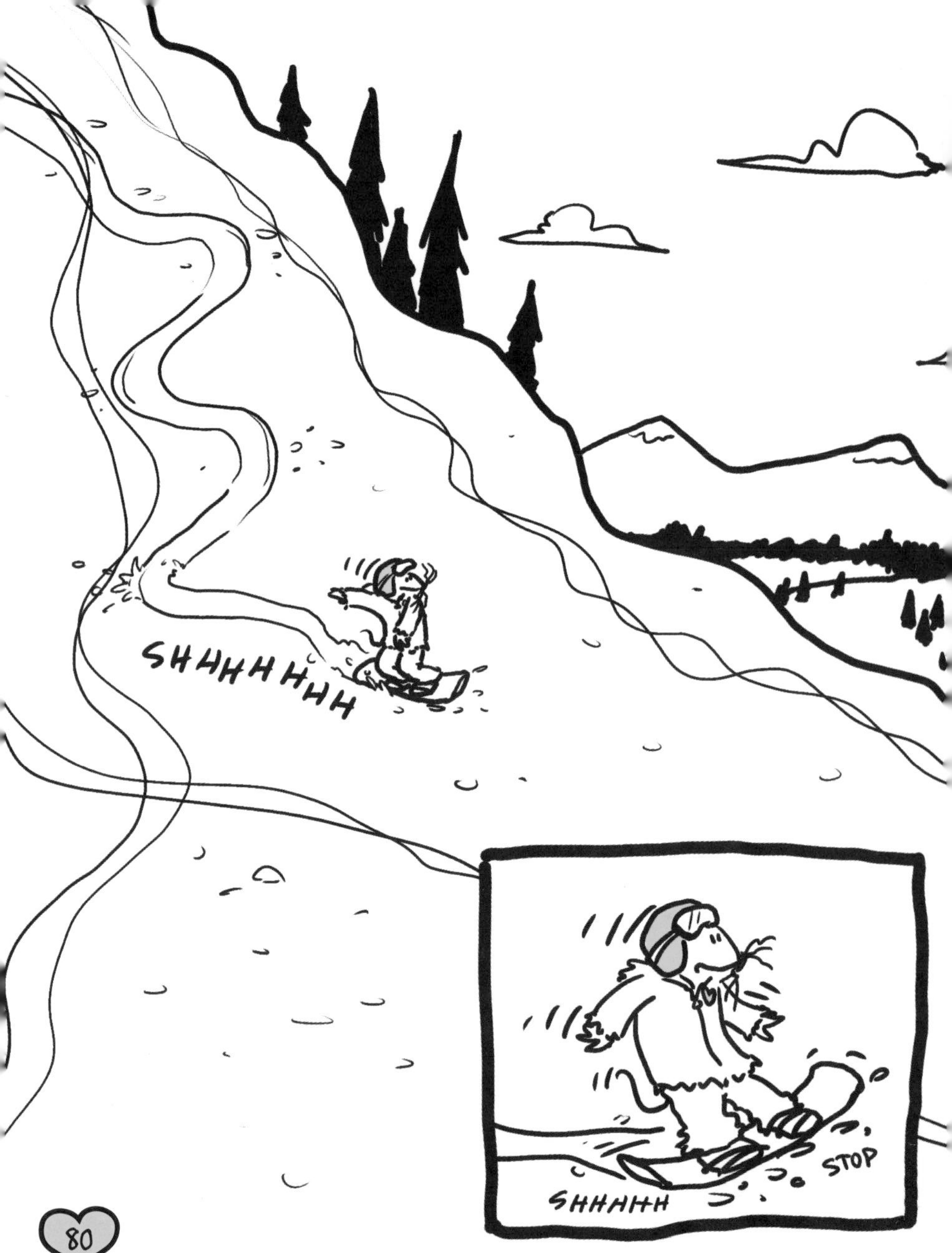
SHHHHHHH
SHHHHH
STOP

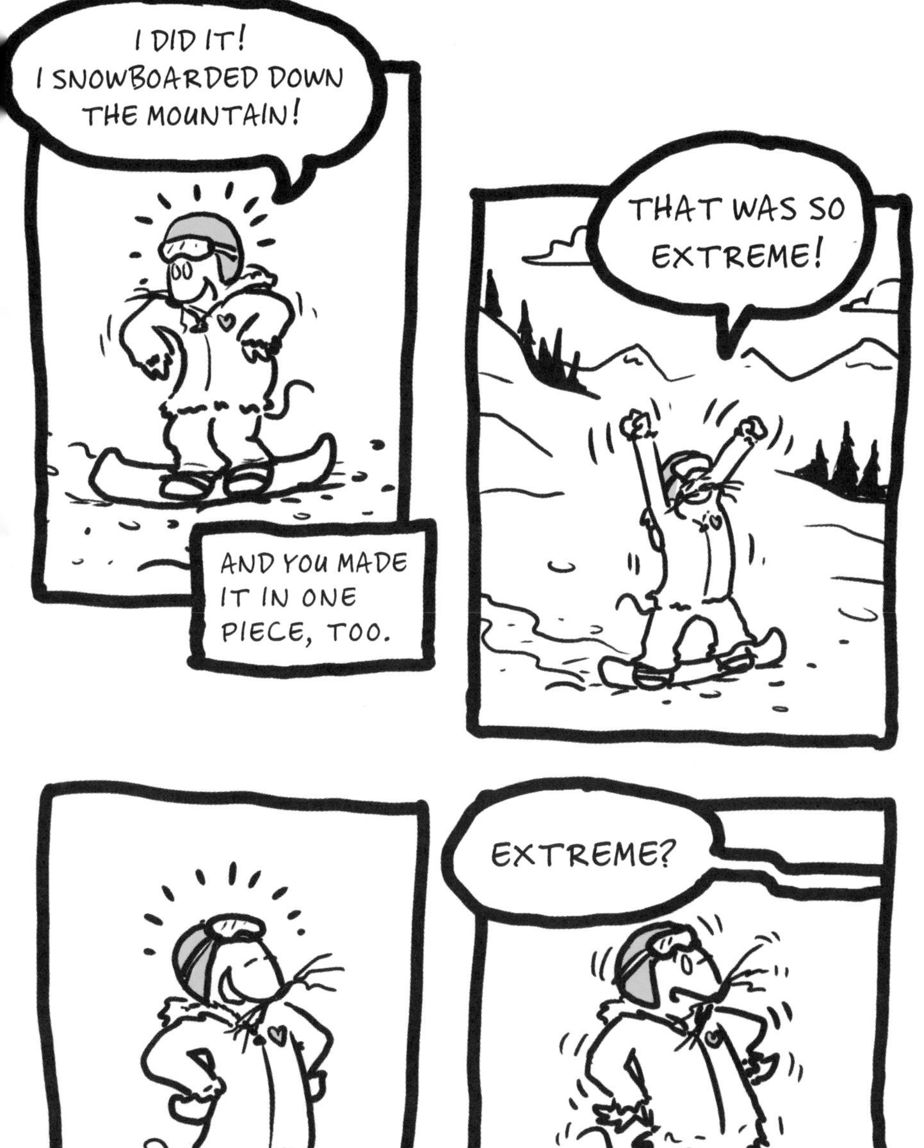
I DID IT! I SNOWBOARDED DOWN THE MOUNTAIN!
AND YOU MADE IT IN ONE PIECE, TOO.
THAT WAS SO EXTREME!
EXTREME?

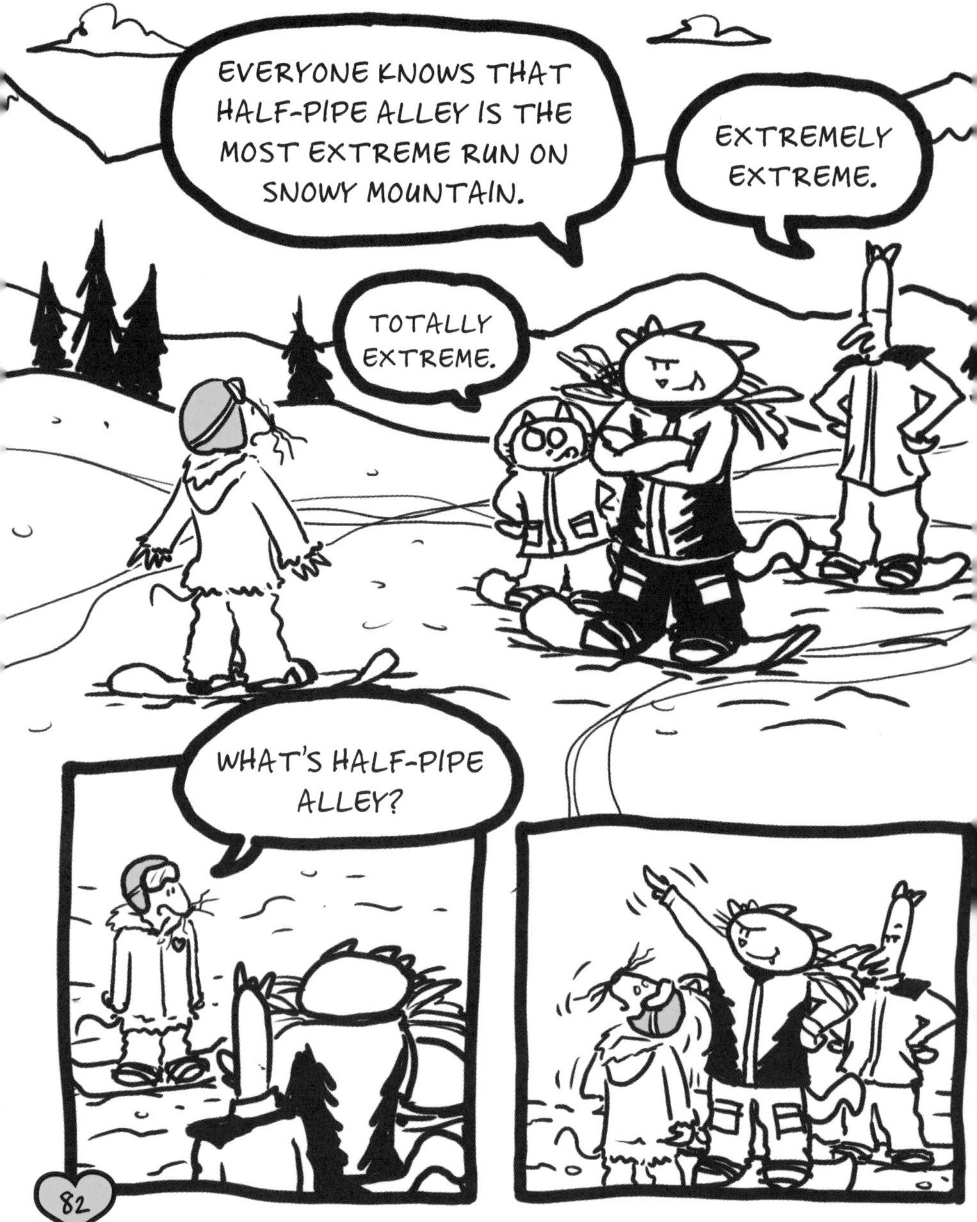
EVERYONE KNOWS THAT HALF-PIPE ALLEY IS THE MOST EXTREME RUN ON SNOWY MOUNTAIN.
EXTREMELY EXTREME.
TOTALLY EXTREME.
WHAT'S HALF-PIPE ALLEY?

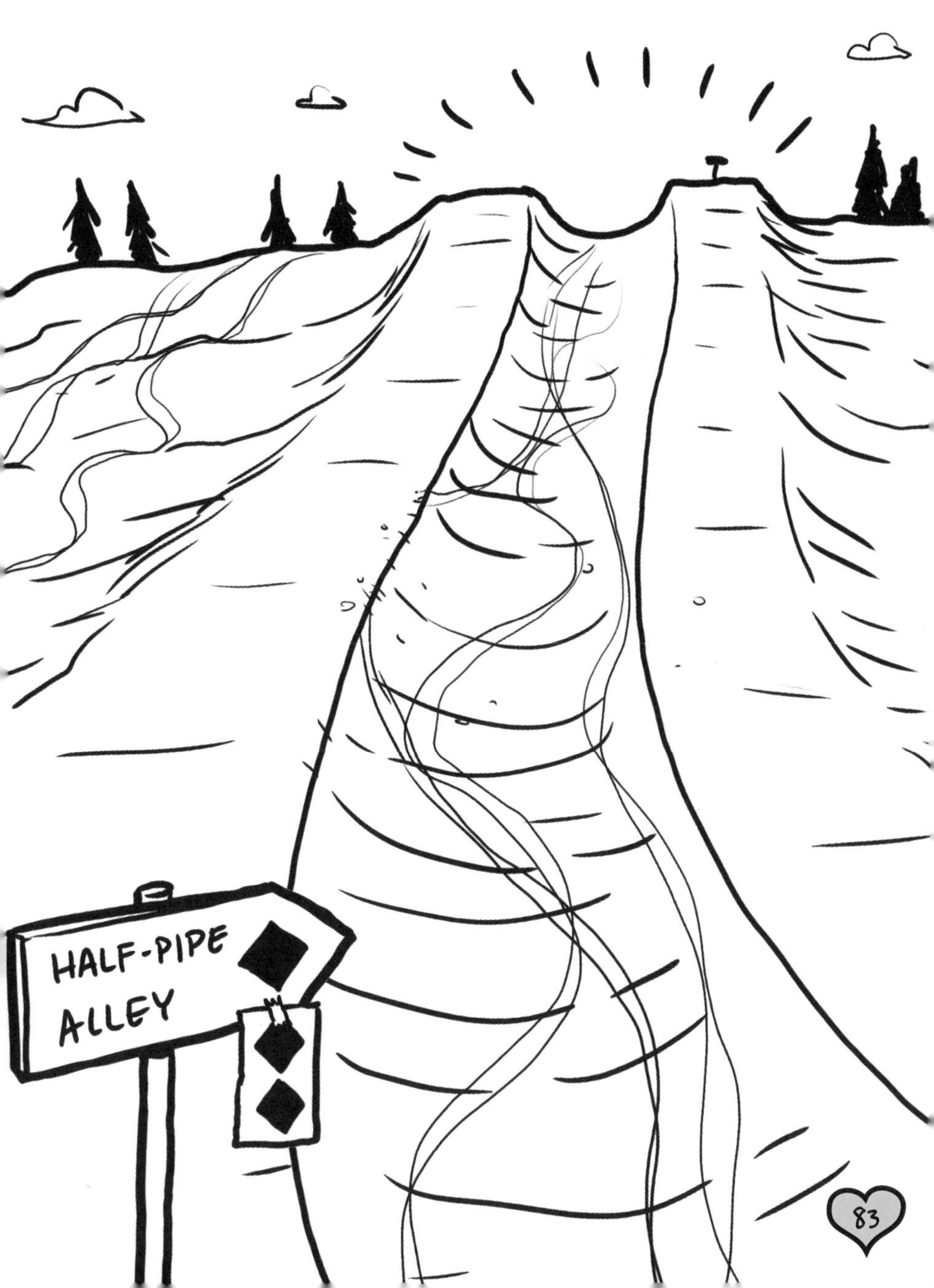
HALF-PIPE
ALLEY

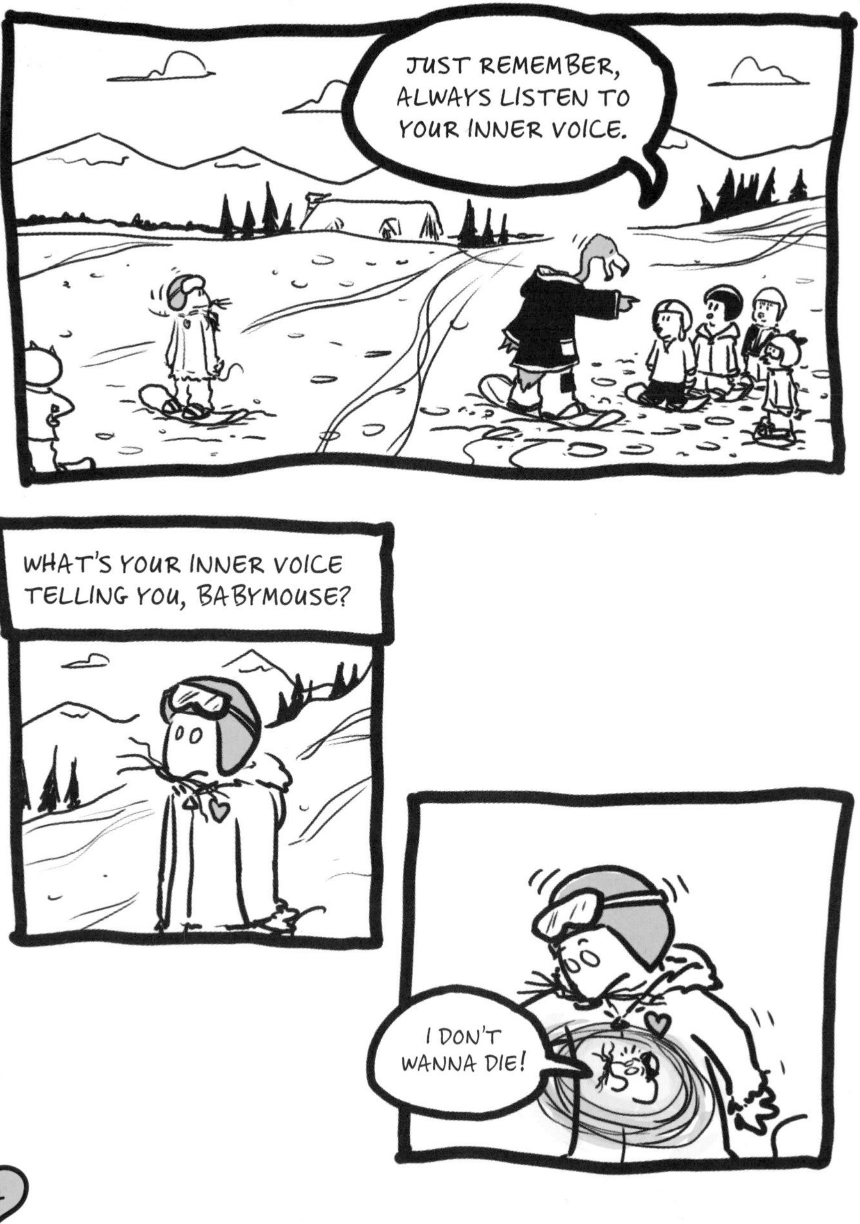
JUST REMEMBER, ALWAYS LISTEN TO YOUR INNER VOICE.
WHAT'S YOUR INNER VOICE TELLING YOU, BABYMOUSE?
I DON'T WANNA DIE!

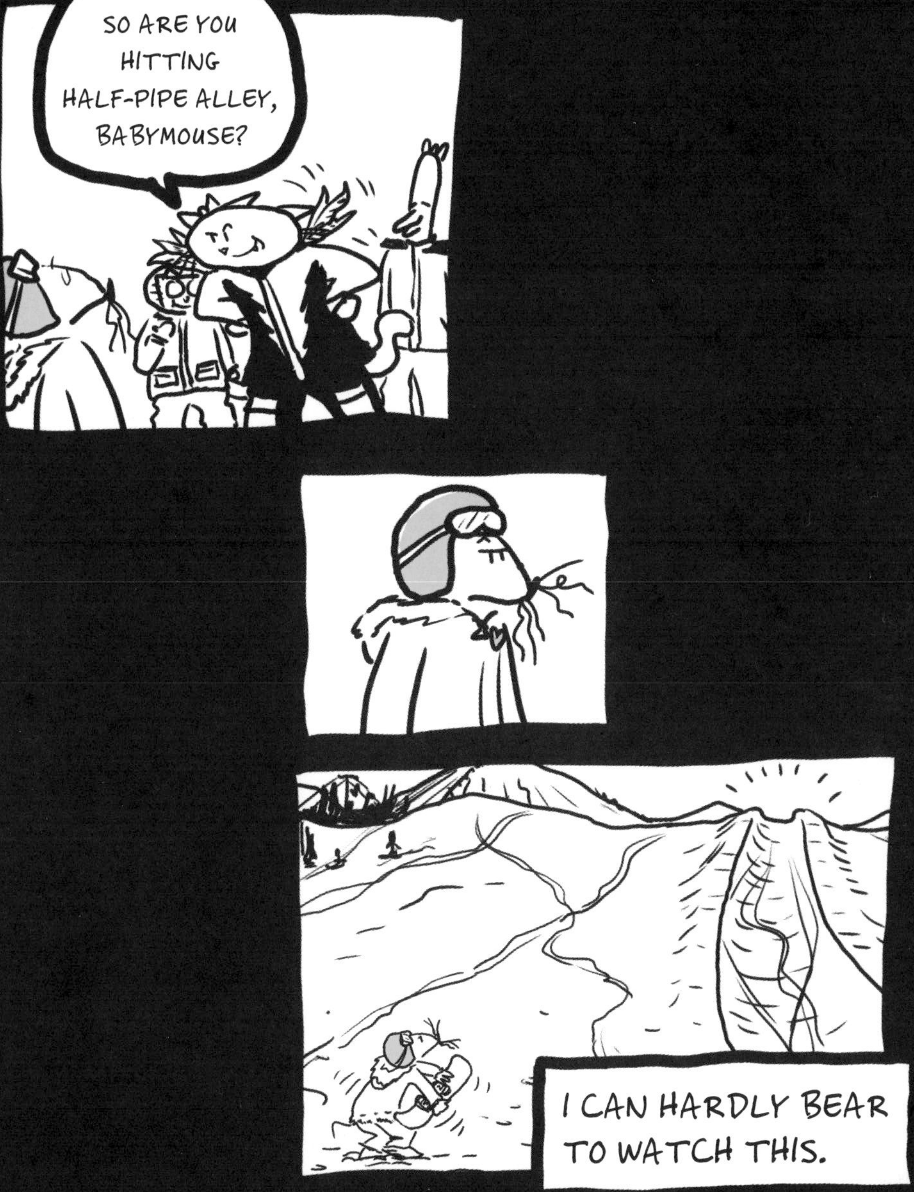
SO ARE YOU HITTING HALF-PIPE ALLEY, BABYMOUSE?
I CAN HARDLY BEAR TO WATCH THIS.

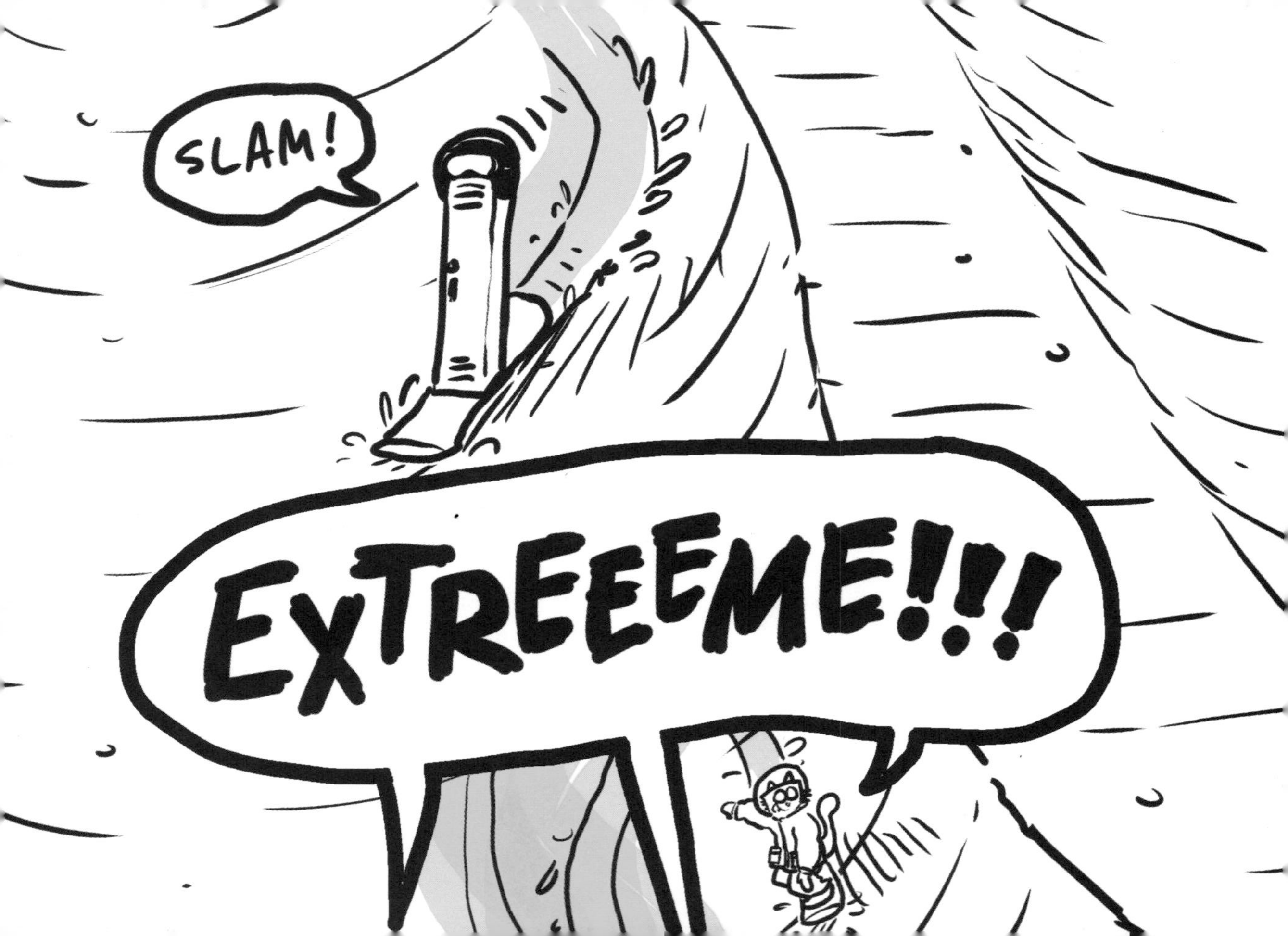
SLAM!
EXTREEEME!!!

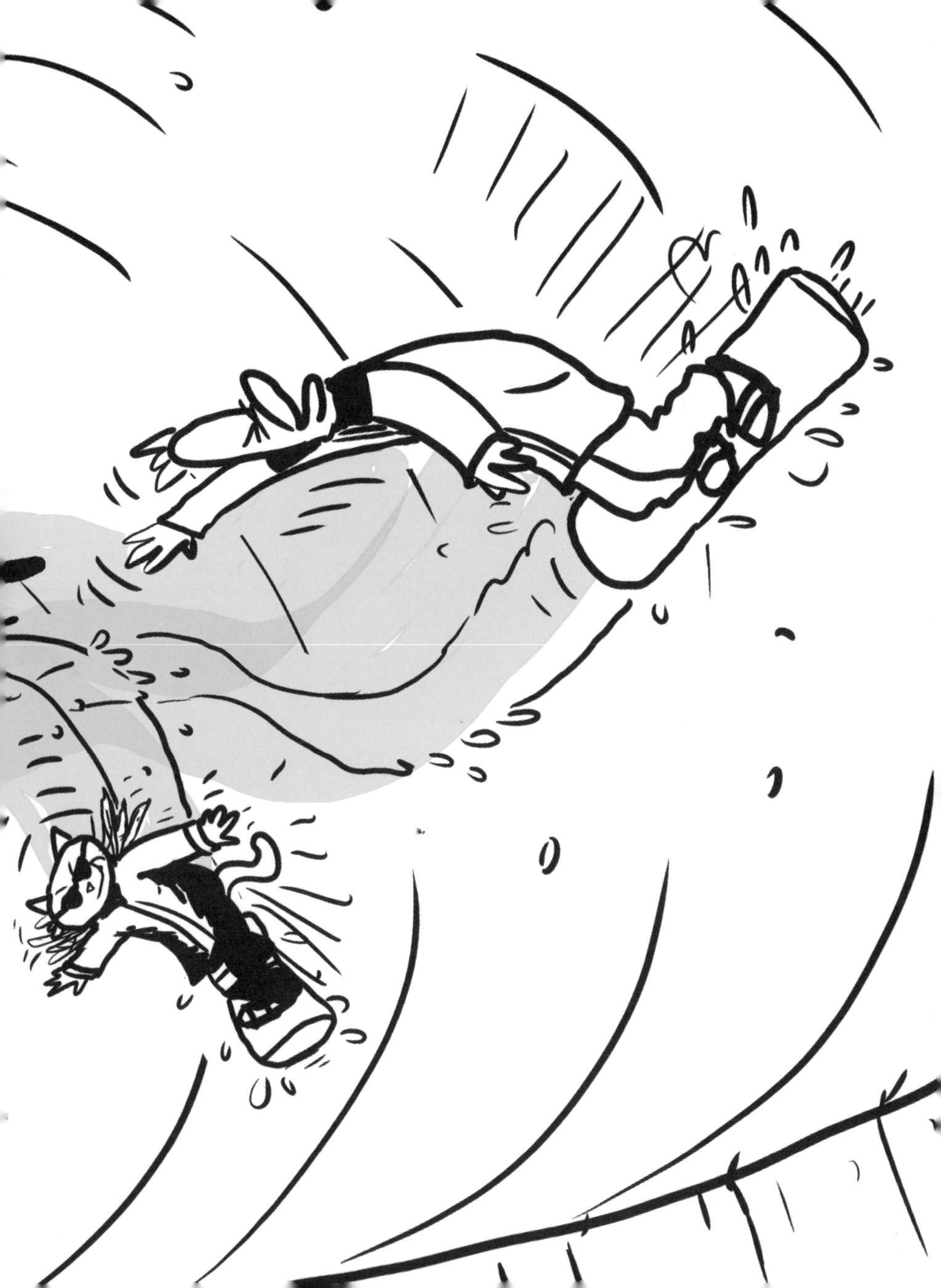

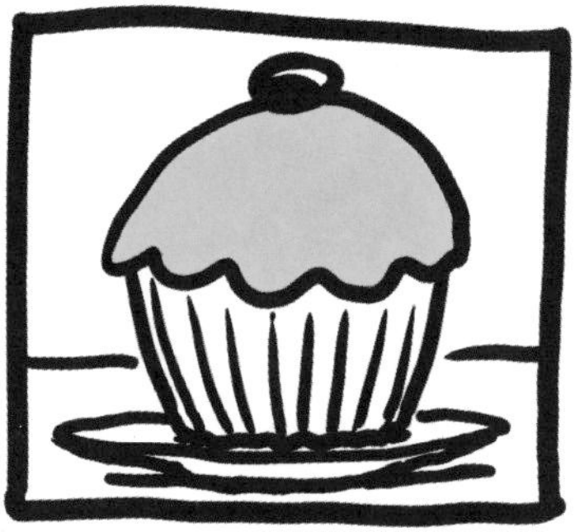

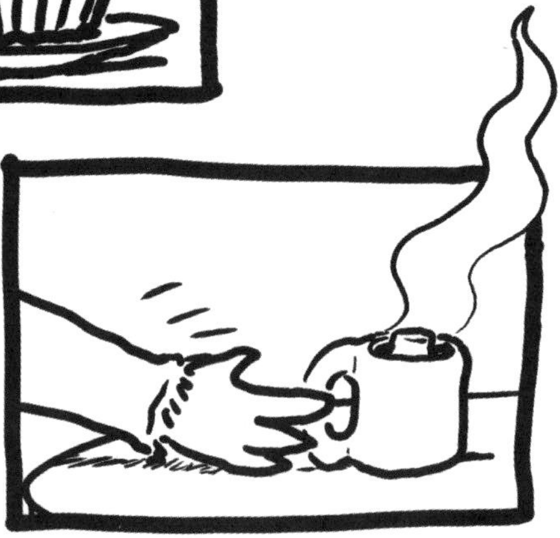

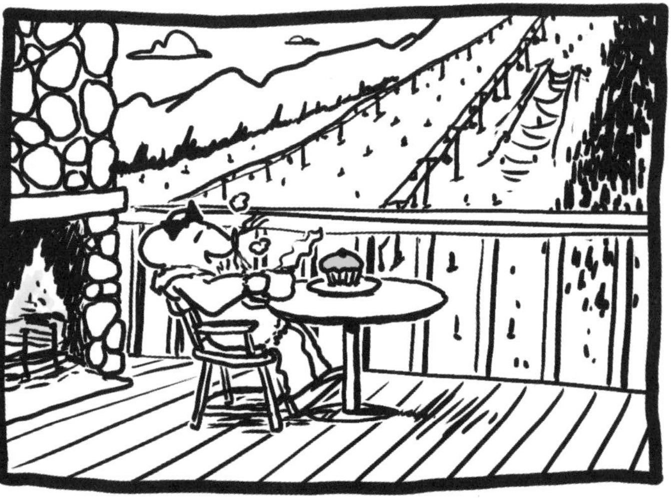

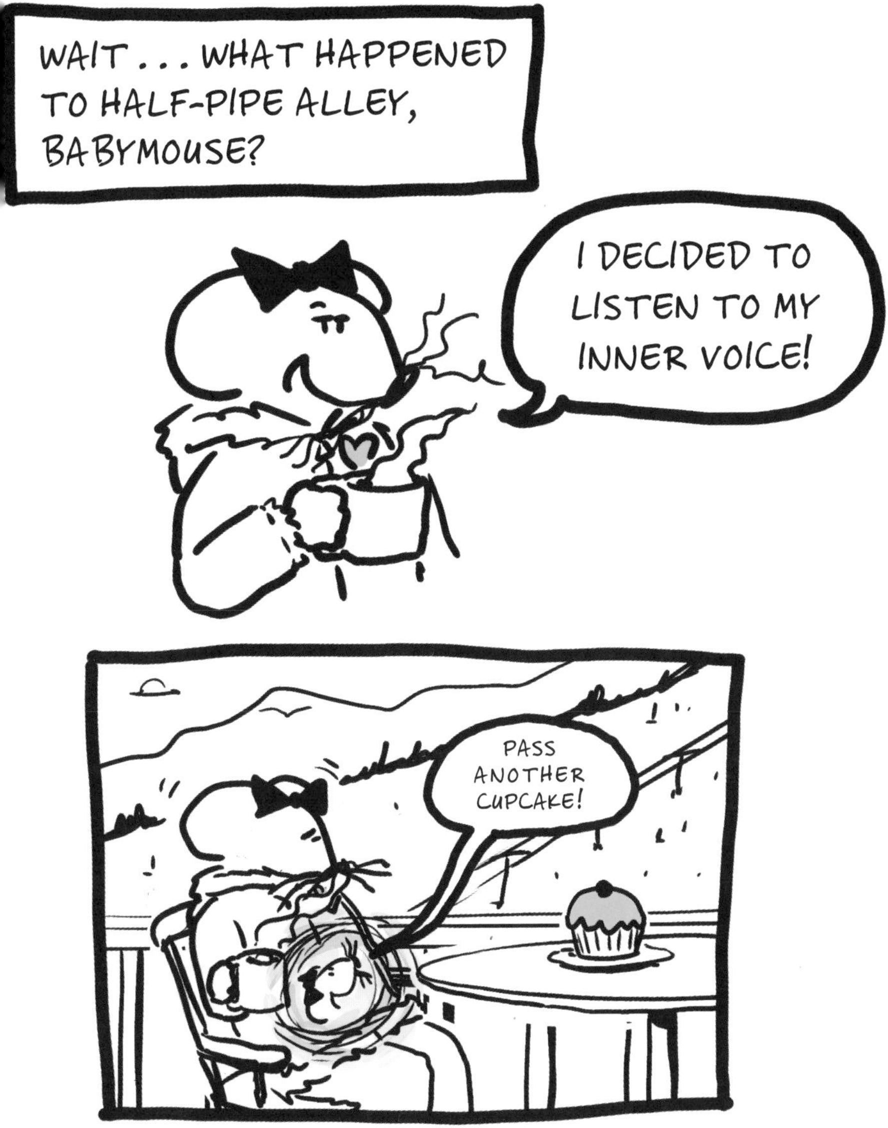
WAIT . . . WHAT HAPPENED TO HALF-PIPE ALLEY, BABYMOUSE?
I DECIDED TO LISTEN TO MY INNER VOICE!
PASS ANOTHER CUPCAKE!

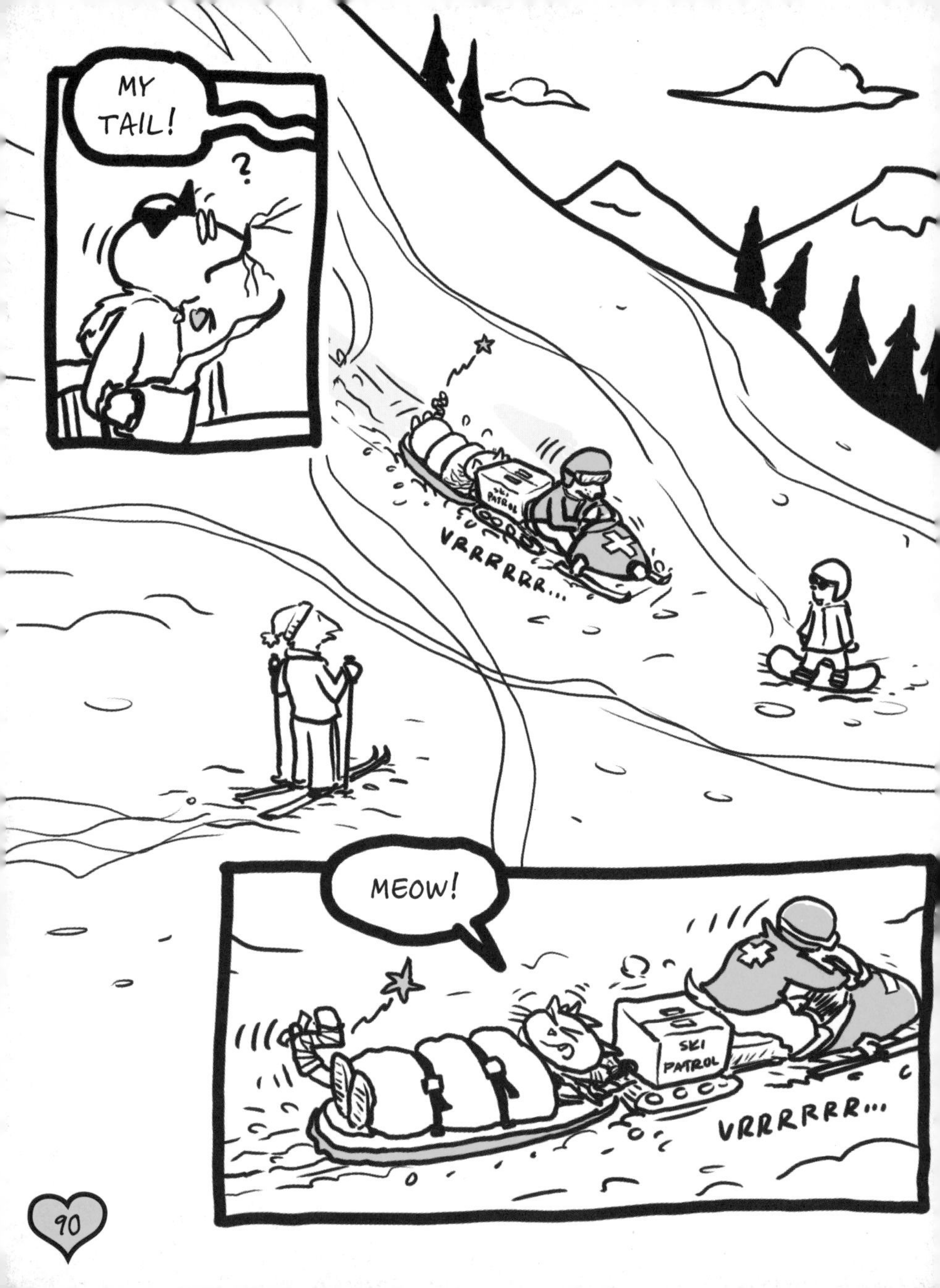
MY TAIL!
?
SKI PATROL
VRRRRRRR...
MEOW!
SKI PATROL
VRRRRRR...

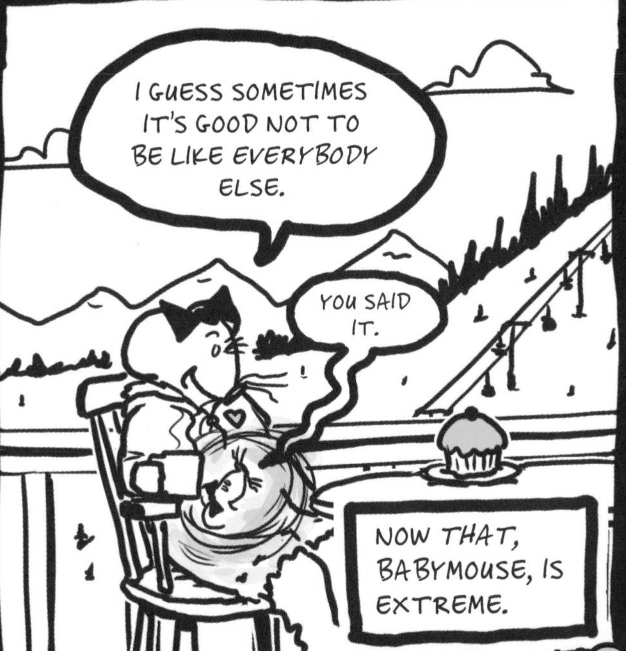
I GUESS SOMETIMES IT'S GOOD NOT TO BE LIKE EVERYBODY ELSE.
YOU SAID IT.
NOW THAT, BABYMOUSE, IS EXTREME.

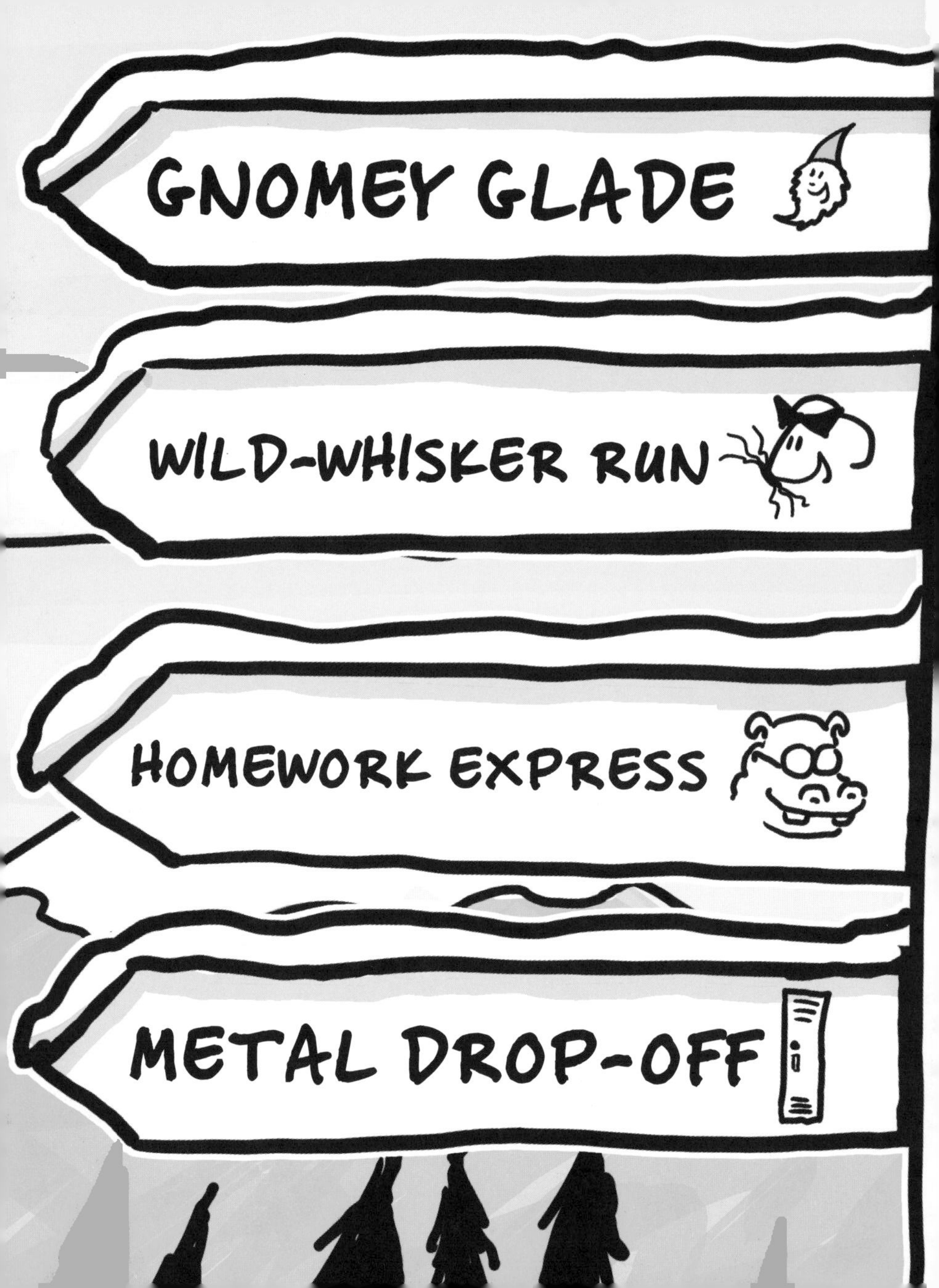
GNOMEY GLADE
WILD-WHISKER RUN
HOMEWORK EXPRESS
METAL DROP-OFF

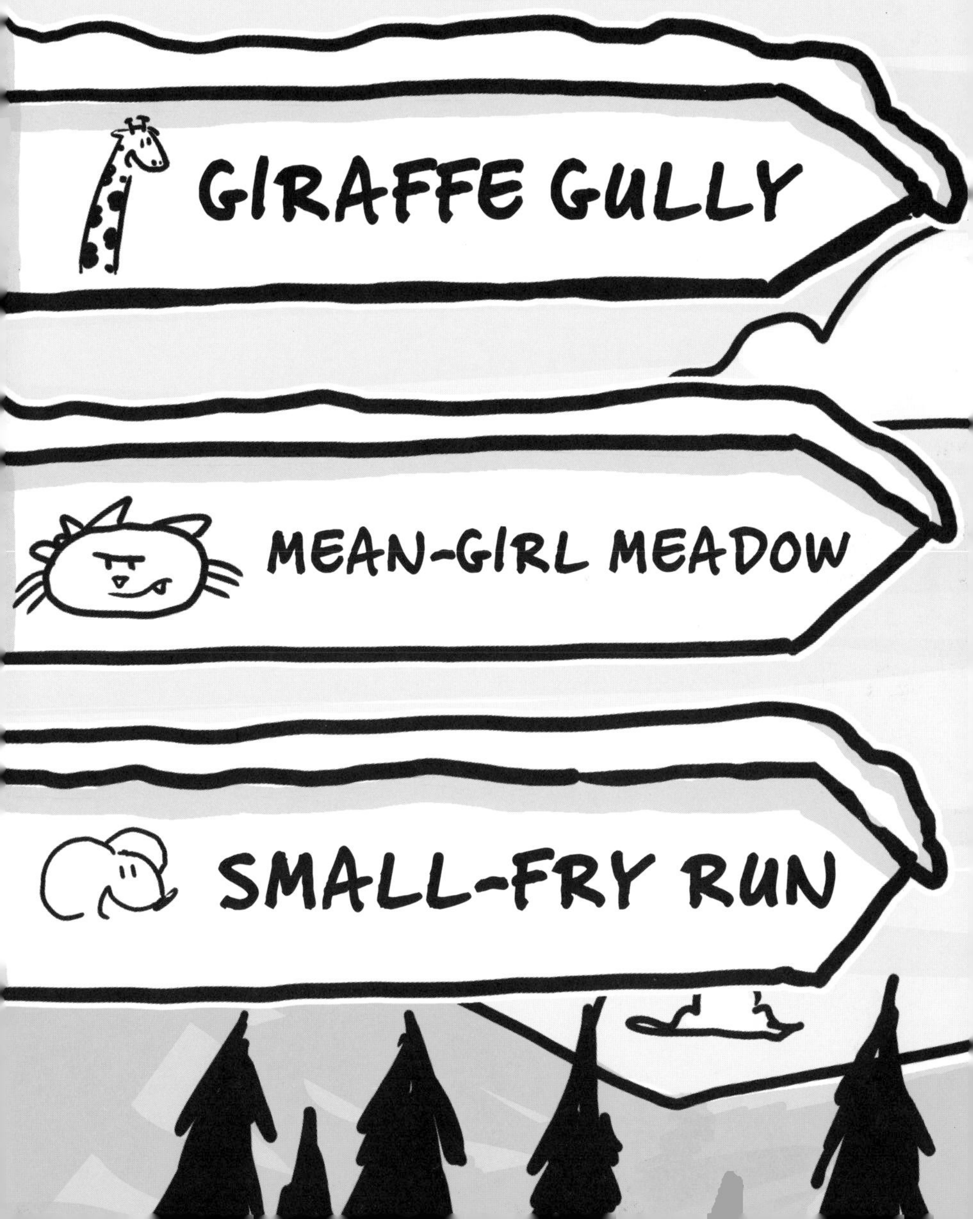
GIRAFFE GULLY
MEAN-GIRL MEADOW
SMALL-FRY RUN

DON'T MISS THE NEXT BABYMOUSE!

HAPPY BIRTHDAY, BABYMOUSE

COMING IN SEPTEMBER 2013

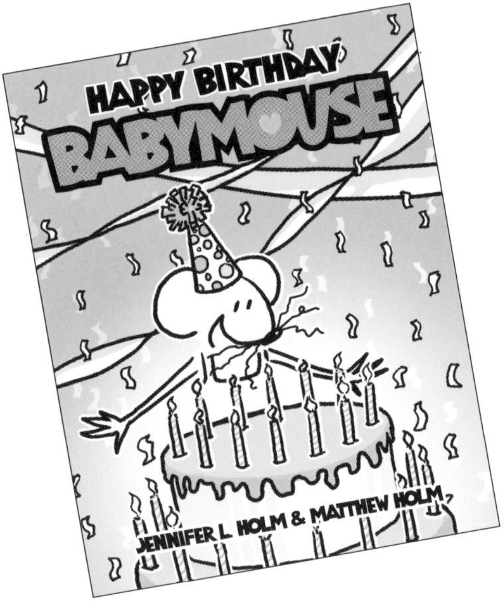
HAPPY BIRTHDAY
BABYMOUSE
JENNIFER L. HOLM & MATTHEW HOLM

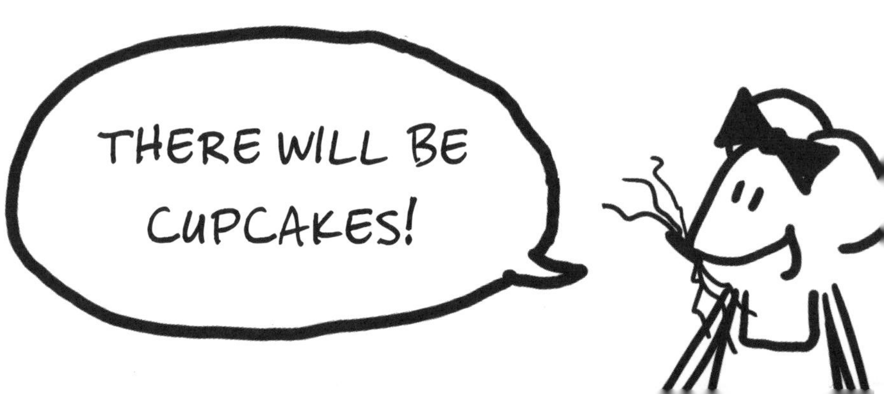
THERE WILL BE CUPCAKES!

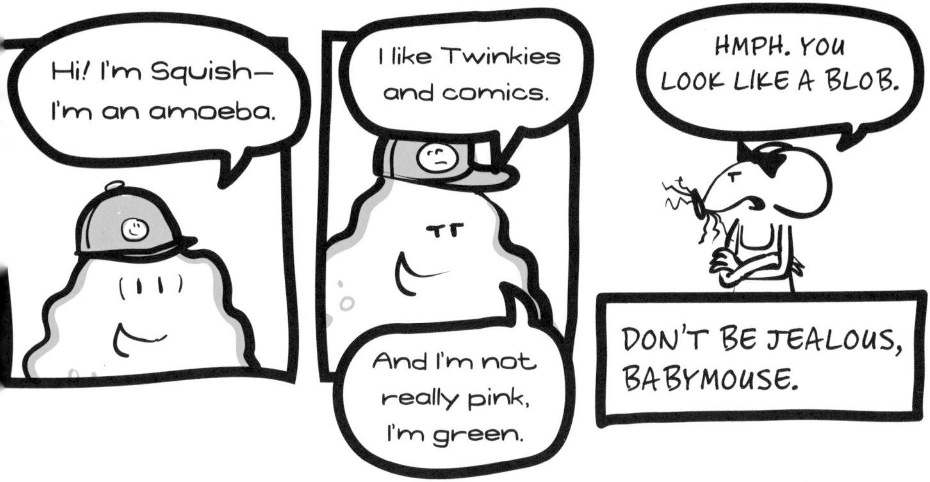
Hi! I'm Squish—
I'm an amoeba.
I like Twinkies and comics.
And I'm not really pink, I'm green.
HMPH. YOU LOOK LIKE A BLOB.
DON'T BE JEALOUS, BABYMOUSE.

READ ABOUT SQUISH'S AMAZING ADVENTURES IN:

#1 SQUISH: Super Amoeba

#2 SQUISH: Brave New Pond

#3 SQUISH: The Power of the Parasite

#4 SQUISH: Captain Disaster

AND COMING SOON:

#5 SQUISH: GAME ON!

★ "IF EVER A NEW SERIES DESERVED TO GO VIRAL, THIS ONE DOES."
—*KIRKUS REVIEWS*, STARRED

If you like Babymouse,
you'll love these other great books
by Jennifer L. Holm!

THE BOSTON JANE TRILOGY

EIGHTH GRADE IS MAKING ME SICK

MIDDLE SCHOOL IS WORSE THAN MEATLOAF

OUR ONLY MAY AMELIA

PENNY FROM HEAVEN

TURTLE IN PARADISE

THEY'RE REALLY GOOD! TRUST ME!